FATAL FESTIVITIES

A DUNE HOUSE COZY MYSTERY
BOOK TWENTY-THREE

CINDY BELL

D1247592

CHAPTER 1

*S*uzie Allen peered at the assortment of dishes that filled the shelves of the solid oak cabinet.

"Do you think we should break out the fine china for this event?" She glanced over her shoulder at Mary Brent as she swept a broom toward the back door. "We'll need it out again soon enough for Thanksgiving."

"I don't know. Will it go with all the sand that Pilot has been tracking in?" Mary laughed as she opened the back door and attempted to sweep out the sand that the boisterous yellow Labrador always seemed to traipse into the house. "I just mopped these floors."

"He always comes back from the beach covered in sand." Suzie closed the cabinet.

"I can't believe Thanksgiving is just around the corner. Or maybe I just don't want to believe it." Mary sighed. "It's not going to be the same without the kids. I know they have busy lives now, but I sure do miss them."

Mary's children, Ben and Cathy, were in their twenties and had recently finished college.

"You'll see them soon enough." Suzie smiled. "I'm sure of it."

"Maybe. I just don't know when." Mary looked over at Suzie. "But it will still be a wonderful holiday, since I get to spend it with you. However, I don't think it's worth getting all the china out for tonight. I think our guests will be happy with the usual plates."

"You're right, we should keep it casual. It just seems like such a special time for our guests. Can you imagine being in your seventies and going on a trip together with all of your friends?" A dreamy smile crossed Suzie's lips. "I think it would be wonderful."

"I don't know how adventurous I'll feel in twenty years." Mary closed the back door and tucked the broom into the storage closet. "But I can tell you that if I'm going anywhere, it's going to be with you."

"You know it!" Suzie grinned. "There's no adventure without the two of us together. But where would we go? Maybe out of the country? There were so many wonderful places I visited when I was an investigative journalist, but I never really had the time to actually experience them. I'd love to be able to go back and just explore."

"That sounds lovely to me." Mary glanced at the clock on the stove. "The bus should be here any minute. I just hope that everyone is as excited as we are."

"I'm sure they will be. It's kind of freeing, isn't it?" Suzie picked up a tray of crackers and cheese that she had put together for the guests to snack on. "Being at an age where you don't have anything to hold you back, all of your responsibilities are in the past, you're retired. If you've had kids, they're grown and living their lives, so all that's left to do is have fun." She carried the tray into the dining room.

"I suppose." Mary followed after her. "But that's only if you have good friends to spend it with. I imagine it would be pretty lonely if you had to navigate all of that freedom alone, not to mention the health issues that sometimes come with it." She gave one of her knees a light slap.

"True." Suzie set the tray down on the long, wooden table that paralleled a wall of floor-to-ceiling windows in the dining room, interrupted only by a sliding glass door. "Luckily, we don't have to worry about the lonely part. The only difficulty we'll have to face is whether or not we take Paul and Wes with us!"

"Oh, good question." Mary laughed. "I don't know how well those two would travel."

"We won't know until we find out, right?" Suzie smiled as she met Mary's eyes. "But maybe we shouldn't wait too long?"

"Well, if we have to leave them behind, we can take Pilot with us." Mary laughed as she glanced toward the dog that was curled up in his dog bed by the window. "He might be a better travel companion."

"Maybe." Suzie looked toward the front door at the sound of a bus pulling into the parking lot. "But for now, we have a B&B to run."

"I'm so glad they decided to have a caterer come in to help us out with the dinner. Between getting all of the guests settled, and arranging the activities for tomorrow, it will make everything so much easier." Mary scrunched up her nose. "Especially since there were so many demands about the meal. I understand it's their annual Thanksgiving dinner, and a special birthday celebration as well, but the requests were a little over the top."

"I agree. The moment they started talking about lobster sauce, I knew we would have been in over our heads." Suzie laughed as she walked toward the door. "Luckily, Tasha came to our rescue. They wanted to use her services. I'm sure she'll do a fantastic job with the meal. Look, she's just pulled up." She pointed to a large, white van that rolled into the parking lot a few seconds after the bus parked.

"Great, everything is going smoothly so far." Mary grabbed Suzie's hand as they reached the edge of the front porch and turned to face her. "We've got this."

"Yes, we do." Suzie smiled as she gazed back at her.

They both took a deep breath, then descended the front steps to welcome the guests who spilled out of the open doors of the bus.

A young woman with her long, brown hair wound into a tight bun on the top of her head, and a clipboard clutched against her chest, tried to get the attention of the others.

"Shady Village residents, please listen up!"

The others continued to mill about and chat with one another.

"I can smell the ocean."

"Look at that gorgeous, old house. I hope they haven't ruined it with updates. You know how people are these days."

"I'm not so sure about all of this sand. It's going to ruin my shoes."

"Does it look like rain to you? It looks like rain to me. Just our luck, we finally get to go on vacation, and it's going to rain!"

The younger woman sighed and raised a megaphone to her mouth. Suzie could see from her name tag that her name was Lorraine Porter, the person who organized the event.

"Shady Village, listen up, please!"

"You'd better put that thing away before I take it from you." The shortest woman in the group started to step toward her.

"Settle down, Beryl." A larger man wrapped his arm around her shoulders. "She's just being enthusiastic."

"Awful, she's being awful." Another woman with

a colorful feather boa wrapped around her neck, covered her ears.

"Line up. Line up, everyone. We need to do a head count." Lorraine shouted her words into the loudspeaker.

The tallest of the women turned to glare at the woman holding the loudspeaker.

"We're all here, Lorraine! We've all been here the whole time. We've been stuck on a bus for hours. Where else would we be?"

"Vera, please just line up." Lorraine gestured to the line. "We're trying to make a good impression and have a nice trip."

"Then put that awful thing away!" The woman who wore the feather boa waved her hand through the air. She had a petite frame but a strong voice. "We're not all deaf, but if you keep using that thing we're going to be!"

"Okay, okay, Greta." Lorraine lowered the megaphone. "I just want to be sure that everyone can hear what I'm saying."

"We can hear you!" The man, who had calmed Beryl took a step toward Lorraine.

"What?" Another man who stood close to him peered at Lorraine. "What did you say? Is it time to eat, Chip?"

"No, John, we just got here." Chip patted his shoulder.

"Actually, we do have some food set out in the dining room, if anyone is hungry." Suzie stepped forward as she assessed the group. She noticed that the third man in the group kept to himself, his eyes glued to his phone. There were a few people talking to each other, but the rest seemed to keep their distance. She wondered if perhaps they weren't all friends after all. "Would everyone like to come inside?" She gestured toward the front porch.

"Oh, I'd love to, but I don't think I'm going to make it up those stairs." A woman in the group leaned heavily on her cane. "I thought this place was accessible?"

"We have a ramp right over here." Mary gestured to the opening for the ramp not far from the stairs. "You and I can both use it. My knees aren't fond of the stairs." She offered a warm smile to the woman.

"Oh, sweetheart, I remember when my knees worked." The woman started toward the ramp. "I didn't know how lucky I was."

"Stop making a fuss, Margret!" Greta glared at her. "We all know your legs are just fine, you just want to be able to get ahead of the group."

"What a terrible thing to say!" Margret turned around to look at Greta. "You can't imagine how much I suffer. Some sister you are." Her gray curls bounced against her shoulders as she turned back to the ramp and continued up it.

Suzie bit the tip of her tongue as she sensed the animosity between the two sisters. She guessed that the bus ride hadn't exactly been pleasant. She had pictured a group of adventurous seniors eager to have a great time, but as far as she could tell, some of them weren't actually thrilled to be there together.

CHAPTER 2

*a*s the rest of the group filed into Dune House, using the front stairs, Suzie noticed the bus driver step out of the bus. He pulled his cap off and sighed.

"I bet you could use some refreshments, too." Suzie smiled at him as she read his name tag. Freddy Bledsoe. "Do you want to come inside? I have fresh lemonade and iced tea, or I can make you a hot drink if you want, Freddy."

"After that trip, I think I'm going to need something a little stronger." Freddy shook his head. "But thanks for the offer. I have to get to my motel and check in. I just need to stretch my legs a little."

"I understand. If you need anything, feel free to contact me. I know just about everyone around here. I'm Suzie, and I run Dune House with my friend, Mary." Suzie pointed in Mary's direction.

"Thank you." Freddy smiled, then walked off.

As he did, Suzie turned to greet the caterer as she approached the porch. "Tasha. I'm so glad you're here."

"Me, too." Tasha grinned at another woman who trailed a few steps behind her. "This is my assistant, Katrina. She'll be helping me get everything ready for dinner."

"Oh yes, we've met before." Suzie smiled. "I think the last time I saw you was at the fundraiser for the hospital last month?"

"Yes. It's nice to see you, again. I hear so many great things about Dune House, but I don't think I've ever been inside." Katrina peered at the building.

"I'd offer to give you a tour, but I need to get the guests settled right now. Once things quiet down, I'll show you around." Suzie glanced toward the van. "Do you need help unloading anything?"

"Not at all. We're here to do the work, remember?" Tasha patted her shoulder, then started to walk back toward the van. "Everything should be ready to go by five o'clock."

"Wonderful, thanks so much!" Suzie turned

toward the steps as the large bus pulled out of the parking lot. She watched it roll down the road. As she looked after it in the direction of the dock, she wondered if Paul was back from his fishing trip. Despite being with him for some time, she still hadn't been able to stop worrying when he was out on the water. As much as she loved the ocean, she also respected its ferocity.

A crash inside the house sent her racing for the door.

"Everyone, stand back! Watch for glass!" Mary's strong voice carried through the dining room into the entranceway.

Suzie spotted the disaster, a shattered vase spread along with a bouquet of flowers across the tile floor.

"I'm so sorry, but he frightened me." The man who had been focused on his phone earlier, looked up at Suzie with a gasp. "I didn't expect there to be a dog!"

"Oh dear, you're not hurt, are you?" Suzie took his hand as she looked him over from head to toe.

"No, I'm not hurt. Just embarrassed." His cheeks flushed as he pulled his hand away. "You really shouldn't have a dog in here."

"Pipe down, Dan!" Margret huffed. "Nothing wrong with having a dog around."

"Pilot is a part of our family. We are very careful to make sure our guests are aware of him being here. It's included in the paperwork that you signed." Suzie softened her voice. "You're not allergic, are you?"

"No, just not accustomed." Dan cleared his throat. "He bolted right past me, and I knocked into the table and brushed the vase off with my elbow. Of course, I will cover the costs."

"Don't worry about that at all." Suzie steered him away from the mess as Mary arrived with a dustpan and broom. "These things happen. Now that you know he's around, he shouldn't startle you. Are you hungry? There's plenty to eat." She directed him to the dining room table spread with an assortment of crackers, cheeses, and sliced meat.

"Thank you." Dan glanced back at the mess on the floor. "I truly am sorry."

"It's quite all right. I'm sorry that you were startled. Hopefully, the rest of your time here will only be pleasant." Suzie smiled as she patted his arm, then walked over to help Mary.

"I guess things aren't going so smoothly after

all." Mary dumped the remains of the vase into the plastic bag that Suzie held.

"If this is the worst of it, then I'd say we're still in pretty good shape." Suzie smiled at her. "Thanks for doing all the cleanup work. I'll make sure that Pilot is comfortable in the yard. I'll start showing people to their rooms, so they can get their luggage put away." She headed into the kitchen in search of Pilot and dropped the plastic bag into the trash just as Tasha stepped in through the kitchen door with a large box. "Oh, let me help you." She reached for the box and steadied it as Tasha continued through the door.

"Thanks so much. It's not heavy, just bulky." Tasha set it down on the counter. "I can't tell you how much I appreciate you letting me cater here. With my business just starting out, it's great to have the opportunity to serve your guests."

"I'm just so glad that you were available when they specially requested you. I figured you might be all booked up. Oh, there you are." Suzie hooked her finger around Pilot's collar as he slunk out of the stairwell into the kitchen. "I see you regret your choices." She rubbed the top of his head. "We all make mistakes, Pilot."

"He's such a beautiful dog." Tasha gave him a

quick pat. "I've started getting some bookings, but it's slow going since the business is so new. I'm going to do my best to impress you and Mary tonight, as well as all of your guests."

"I have no doubt that you'll succeed." Suzie flashed a quick smile at Katrina as she stepped inside with several cloth bags looped over her arms. "I'll get out of your way so you can get started."

As Suzie guided Pilot out of the kitchen into the hallway, Greta walked toward them.

"Oh, he's so adorable." She grinned widely as she patted his head. "I just love dogs. When I heard there would be a dog here, I was so excited. Do you think I could spend time with him later, after I've settled in?"

"Of course." Suzie smiled. "He has a fenced area out the back. It's all set up for him. I'm just going to take him there now."

"Oh great." Greta looked down at Pilot. "I'll come play ball with you later." The dog's tail wagged with excitement.

"If you can't find him, just let me know. He often spends time in Mary's room." Suzie guided Pilot out the back to the fenced-in yard. As soon as she opened the gate, he ran over to his large dog bed, and flopped down in a comfortable spot.

"There, isn't that better than terrorizing the guests?" Suzie grinned, blew him a kiss, and closed the gate. She walked back into the house.

"May I see my room, please?" Greta appeared at the end of the hallway as Suzie stepped into it. "I'd like to get a few things put away before dinner."

"Of course. I was just going to show everyone to their rooms. I have both you and your sister, Margret, on the first floor." Suzie peered through the kitchen door in the direction of the dining room. "Let me see if anyone else is ready."

"Ugh, I'll have to apologize in advance for my sister. We may be blood, but I definitely do not claim her." Greta followed Suzie into the dining room.

"Did something happen between the two of you that caused so much friction?" Suzie glanced over at her. "Maybe this weekend can be an opportunity to mend the relationship?"

"Not a chance." Greta sighed. "Many, many years ago we were close, but Margret has never been quite right. We have the same parents, but that is our only similarity."

"Is my sister singing my praises?" Margret stepped out of the living room and draped her arm around Greta's shoulders. "She's always so kind." Her voice dripped with dark sarcasm.

Suzie's heart pounded as she sensed the tension increase between the two sisters. She seized the opportunity to change the subject before Greta could respond.

"I was just telling Greta that I'd like to show everyone to their rooms. Would you like to see your room, Margret?" She infused as much warmth into her smile as she could muster.

"Show me the way." Margret tapped her cane against the floor.

CHAPTER 3

*S*uzie led the four guests, who were staying on the first floor, down the hall. She directed each to their room as they passed by the open doors.

As she listened to all of the exclamations over the décor of the rooms, she felt a buzz of excitement. She'd spent a lot of time designing each room with its own unique theme and regularly changed the designs. She always appreciated when the guests were thrilled to see them. With quite a large group, she'd sent pictures to them before they arrived, so they could pick out which rooms they preferred. With a few rooms to spare, everyone who had chosen a room had managed to pick their favorite.

"This is the room I picked!" A shrill voice carried from the other end of the hall.

Suzie turned back to see Greta glaring at her sister. "You know it's the room I picked! We talked about it! I love the hot air balloon theme because Peter and I went on one on our honeymoon. I told you that!"

"I don't remember any of that." Margret leaned on her cane and glared back at her sister. "I remember that I picked this room, because I love all of the paintings of the sky that hung in the room. I told you that. I loved the idea of being surrounded by such beauty. I want to feel like I'm flying."

"Ladies, is there a problem?" Suzie approached them with a building sense of dread as each appeared to dig in.

"I reserved this room before we arrived." Greta looked over at her. "Don't you have some kind of record of that?"

Suzie pulled out her phone and looked over the reservations she'd received. Her heart sank. She looked up at them. "I'm so sorry, but it doesn't appear that either of you sent through a room preference. I assumed you wanted to pick when you arrived. We do have a couple of other rooms to choose from. One has a cliff theme with some sky elements included. Would either of you like to see it?"

"I'm scared of heights!" Margret shook her head. "I couldn't possibly wake up and feel like I was on the side of a cliff!"

"Oh, it's not exactly like that. It just involves some rocky décor, and sunrise colors." Suzie gestured to the next door. "Let me show you. You might find that you like it."

"No! Absolutely not. This is the room I reserved, and this is the room I will be staying in." Margret shot a sharp glare at Greta. "There's nothing you can do about it!"

"One minute you want to feel like you're flying, the next you're scared of heights. You knew I wanted this room. That's the only reason you're doing this." Greta blinked back tears. "I still don't know how you managed to weasel your way on to this trip and make it all about you! Nothing you do should surprise me anymore!"

"I also have a Paris-themed room." Suzie's heart raced as she sensed that if the argument wasn't stopped, it would continue to escalate. "Do either of you like Paris?"

"I'll take the cliff room." Greta sighed and opened the door to the neighboring room. "Just let

Margret have the room I picked. There's no point in fighting it. She always wins."

"Stop being a baby." Margret waved her hand through the air. "I picked this room fair and square, and you know it."

"I don't know that at all." Greta whipped around to face her sister. "But I don't have the energy to fight with you. So, have your room and enjoy it. But don't expect me to be at your birthday celebration. I won't be there." She stepped into the cliff-themed room and slammed the door shut behind her.

"I'm so sorry about the mix-up." Suzie turned toward Margret, only to see a door swinging toward her face. As it slammed shut, she jerked back.

She'd spent a little time early that morning picturing how the day would go. This certainly had not been her prediction. With her heart in her throat, she led the rest of the guests upstairs to their rooms.

"Don't worry about those two." Vera strolled into her room and smiled at the assortment of art and decorations that depicted the streets of an Italian city. "They are always at each other's throats."

"But why?" Suzie felt some relief that the rest of the guests seemed to be satisfied with their accommodations. "What terrible thing turned them against each other this way?"

"It wasn't just one thing. Some stories are better left untold." Vera closed the door to her room.

Suzie took a deep breath and tried to focus on the fact that the majority of the guests were enjoying their rooms, and their trip. As she walked back down the stairs into the kitchen, she saw Mary near the sink.

"Everyone's settled in their rooms." Suzie descended the last step, then leaned against the counter beside Mary. "I'm not so sure this is going to be a smooth weekend."

"Me, neither." Mary straightened up and looked over at her. "There are all kinds of rumors flying around that Margret and Greta are going to end up in quite a catfight before the end of the trip. From what I overheard, bets have been placed as to who the victor will be."

"We'll have to do our best to prevent that from happening. The last thing we need is a big fight. We can get them through this. Maybe some time away from their usual routine, in a beautiful place like this, will rekindle their connection."

"Maybe. We can hope." Mary stepped to the

side as Tasha hurried past them with a stack of platters.

"Are you sure we can't help?" Suzie watched her attempt to balance the platters while making room on the counter.

"The only way you can help is to stay out of the kitchen." Tasha flashed them a wide grin. "I need all the space I can get!"

"No problem!" Mary took a step back from the counter and smiled. "I'm glad to get out of your hair."

"We can get the table set up for dinner." Suzie picked up a wooden box of silverware. "Lorraine gave us a seating map, so we can do place cards. I think it's to prevent drama from brewing."

"Probably." Mary grabbed some note cards from a drawer. "The question is, do any of them get along?"

"I'm quite certain that we're going to find out." Suzie looked over at two men who walked through the entranceway in the direction of the dining room.

"If those two don't stop bickering, I'm not getting back on the bus with them." John scowled as he continued toward the dining room. "I didn't pay for this trip to endure their petty little fights."

"Relax, John, they're old, one of them will kick

the bucket soon enough." Chip clapped his shoulder and smiled.

"We're old, too, Chip." John chuckled. "Remember? I don't want my last moments on earth to be spent listening to those two squabbling."

"Dinner will be served in just a little while." Suzie smiled as she greeted them both. "Until then, the side porch has a beautiful view of the water and plenty of comfortable chairs to relax in." She gestured to the glass doors that led out onto the wraparound porch.

"That sounds wonderful, as long as they aren't out there." John peered through the doors, then opened one and stepped out.

"Sorry about John." Chip tilted his head toward him as he settled in one of the lounge chairs. "He gets a little worked up when Greta and Margret go at each other. I'm sure once we've all had a chance to settle, things will calm down."

"Absolutely. It was a long trip, and everyone needs a chance to relax and get refreshed. Let me know if you two would like any drinks out there." Suzie gestured to the kitchen. "I can bring a tray out."

"Don't worry yourself about that. We'll be just

fine." Chip stepped out through the door and closed it behind him.

"See?" Suzie began to sort through the silverware. "There is so much tension between those sisters, it's going to cast a shadow over this entire weekend. You should have seen the way they were arguing."

"It sounds like you did your best to diffuse the situation, Suzie." Mary finished folding the last of the napkins. "You can't expect everyone to get along all of the time."

"No, but this was really vicious. They seem to hate each other." Suzie set out silverware on top of the napkins. "I think that they are going to feud for the whole stay."

"They'll probably cool down. Sisters usually work things out. We always do." Mary winked at her. "We might not be sisters by blood, but we are sisters in every other way."

"True." Suzie smiled.

"It looks like everyone is heading back from exploring." Mary looked toward the sliding glass doors that faced the beach.

"Everything is just about ready!" Tasha called out from the kitchen.

"Perfect timing." Suzie smiled. "They had

wanted to eat at around five. It seems too early to me, but I guess they don't want to go to bed on a full stomach."

"It's a Thanksgiving and birthday dinner, everyone will be celebrating. It'll change the mood, and everyone will have a great time." Mary gestured around her. "Soon enough Dune House will be the go-to option for group travel, and we'll never have an empty room."

"That sounds exhausting." Suzie laughed. "But good."

"I'll round everybody up." Mary opened the door onto the porch and stepped out.

Suzie turned toward the kitchen, eager to see if she could do anything to help.

Katrina stepped through the doorway of the kitchen with her arms full of baskets covered in cloth.

"Let me take some of those." Suzie plucked the baskets from her arms and set them down on the dining room table.

"Thanks, they are hot." Katrina grinned. "Don't they smell delicious? Fresh bread is my favorite smell, I think."

"Absolutely divine! I can't wait to taste some. And all of the other scents coming out of that kitchen are making my mouth water." Suzie eyed the place cards on the table and noticed that Greta's had been set next to John's. She quickly switched it with Vera's, to make sure that John had as much space away from Greta and Margret as possible.

As the guests began to take their seats, she noticed that Greta's chair remained empty. Perhaps she really had decided not to attend the dinner. Suzie made a mental note to check in with her later to see if she needed any food delivered to her room.

Suzie and Mary helped serve the soup and main meal of roast turkey and a large assortment of sides. They had some food to eat in the kitchen between helping Tasha and Katrina serve. It was delicious, and they both decided to definitely use Tasha to cater for future events. As they served the table, they were swept up in the lively conversation of those gathered around it.

Once the main course had been served and cleared, Tasha and Katrina carried a large birthday cake out to the table. From the disgruntled chatter among the guests, when Margret wasn't in the room shortly before the cake was served, Suzie and Mary had learned that apparently Margret had insisted that a birthday cake be served instead of the planned pumpkin pie.

"Oh boy!" Margret clapped her hands as the candles on the cake cast a glow into her eyes. She took a deep breath and blew out the candles. "I wish for another great year."

A few people cheered and wished her a happy birthday as Suzie and Mary watched from the side.

Tasha began slicing the cake. She cut a large hunk for Margret.

"A little extra frosting on mine, please." Margret licked her lips as Tasha set the plate down in front of her.

"A toast!" Vera raised her wineglass high in the air as she looked around the table. "To the birthday girl, thanks for being our excuse to celebrate!"

A smattering of less than enthusiastic applause followed the toast.

Margret pushed herself up from her chair and leaned against the table. Her eyes narrowed, she pursed her lips, and her face got very red. She took a deep breath. Before she could say a single word, she clutched her stomach and fell forward across the table, crushing the large slice of cake that filled her plate.

CHAPTER 4

"*M*argret?" Suzie rushed to her side. "Are you okay?"

Mary rounded the table from the other direction. "Is she choking?"

"She's faking it." Vera rolled her eyes. "She's always looking for some way to get more attention."

"No." Suzie pressed her fingertips against the side of Margret's neck and shuddered. "No, she's not faking it. Mary, call for an ambulance!" She guided Margret's body from the table to the floor. "Margret! Can you hear me?" She shook her shoulders and leaned close in an attempt to detect any breath coming from her mouth or nose. As she launched into chest compressions, the people at the table stood up and gathered around her.

Suzie tuned out the mumbles and whispers that she heard. Even as she attempted to revive Margret, she knew that her attempts were futile. Margret showed no sign of life.

"Suzie, the paramedics are here!" Mary rushed to her side with two paramedics behind her.

Suzie moved aside as the paramedics took over. She rubbed her aching arms as she looked up at Mary and shook her head.

Mary walked around the paramedics and wrapped her arms around Suzie who still kneeled on the floor.

"You did everything you could, Suzie."

"How could this happen?" Suzie looked up at the faces that still surrounded Margret. "Everyone, please, let's go into the living room and give the paramedics some room to work." She stood up even as her mind swirled, then sharpened. Something shocking had happened, but she had to keep it together for the guests.

"Is she dead?" Vera's wide, blue eyes sought deep into Suzie's. "Is she really dead?"

Suzie's heart lurched as she struggled to find an answer for Vera. She doubted that Margret would survive, but she couldn't bring herself to speak the words. Just that morning she'd been expecting to guide a group of seventy-somethings through a wonderful weekend. Now, she was faced with confirming the death of one of them.

Mary guided Vera away from Suzie and directed her to the large easy chair in the living room.

"Let's just sit down here."

"I'll get everyone some tea." Tasha headed out of the living room and back toward the kitchen.

"Tea would be good," Suzie said, her mind still reeling.

"Tea isn't going to change the fact that Margret just dropped dead right in front of us!" Chip paced toward the doorway of the living room. "Are we all just supposed to sit here and sip tea while she's lying there on the floor?"

"I'm so sorry this has happened, Chip." Mary stepped between him and the door. "But the best thing we can do right now is to remain as calm as we can."

"Calm? How are we supposed to stay calm?" Vera stood up. "I knew she would find a way to ruin this trip. First, it was insisting on coming with us, then that we make our Thanksgiving dinner a birthday celebration as well. I thought that would be it. But she went and outdid herself this time."

"Stop it!" John glared in her direction. "Have some respect, Vera! A woman is dead!"

"I didn't mean anything by it." Vera sniffled as she clasped her hands together. "It's just such a shock."

"It's okay." Mary guided Vera back down into the chair. "I know it's a lot to face. We're all going to have a lot of different reactions to it. It's a very unexpected situation."

"Suzie?" A young woman in a medical examiner's jacket stuck her head into the living room. "Jason is on his way, but I was closer."

Suzie felt relief that Dr. Summer Rose was there, and Detective Jason Allen, Suzie's younger cousin, was on the way.

"Summer, thank you so much for coming out so quickly." Suzie led her into the dining room. "I have no idea what happened."

"I'll be a second." Summer spoke to the paramedics as they packed up their supplies. As they started for the door, Summer turned back toward Suzie. "So what happened exactly?"

"It all happened so quickly. She was perfectly fine, then she stood up, grabbed her stomach, turned really red, and collapsed across the table. I moved her to the floor and attempted to revive her, but it didn't work. The paramedics took over, and they didn't have any success, either." Suzie clasped her hands together and squeezed. "It just happened. It was so unexpected. Do you think it might have been a heart attack?"

"I don't know." Summer crouched down beside Margret and studied her face. "I'm going to need to get her to the morgue as soon as possible, but I'm sure Jason will want to evaluate things before I do."

"Yes, I will." Jason stepped into the dining room. "Suzie, are you and Mary all right?"

"Yes. I think she must have had a heart attack."

"From her reaction and the speed of her death, I don't know if this was a heart attack, at least not a natural one." Summer looked up at Jason. She pulled a pouch out of the bag she wore over her shoulder and unzipped it.

"You think foul play might have been involved?" Jason asked.

"I think it's possible, from what Suzie described, that she had a toxin in her system." Summer met Jason's eyes. "I need to run some tests to determine what happened. But from what I can tell so far, we need to treat this as a possible poisoning. A possible targeted poisoning."

"Unbelievable." Jason swept his gaze over

Margret's body, then looked up at Suzie. "As of now, no one should eat or drink anything in this house. Understand?"

"You really think someone poisoned her?" Suzie's heart pounded. "Are you sure?"

"No, not at all." Summer looked around the room. "But we have to be cautious."

"Do you think the poison was in her food?" Suzie gasped.

"It's the easiest way to deliver it. But it's possible it was in something else as well." Summer straightened up.

"But what about the other guests? We were all eating and drinking at the table. Shouldn't someone check on them?" Suzie asked.

"I'll get the paramedics back to evaluate everyone in the house. But if she was poisoned, and it's the kind of poison I think it might be, if other people ingested it, they more than likely would have shown signs quickly." Summer looked over at Suzie.

"The group just arrived this afternoon. None of the other guests have shown any signs of being sick. From what I know, she hasn't left Dune House since her arrival."

"Did she eat anything that no one else did?"

Summer looked over the table. "Where are the dishes from the previous courses?"

"Everything should be in the sink or drying. A caterer hosted the meal." Suzie gasped and looked toward the kitchen. "Tasha? Don't make the tea! Don't drink anything in the kitchen!" Fear ricocheted through her. "Oh no! What if they were poisoned, too?" She lunged toward the kitchen.

Jason grabbed her arm and pulled her back. "I'll check on them. You stay here." His tone hardened, leaving no room for debate.

Suzie held her breath as she watched him disappear into the kitchen.

"Everyone's okay in here!" Jason's voice carried out through the doorway.

Suzie and Mary met eyes as they both sighed with relief.

Jason stepped back out of the kitchen with Tasha and Katrina following behind him.

"Is everyone here?" He looked over the group gathered in the living room.

"No." The fog began to clear from Suzie's mind as she focused on the faces assembled before her. "Lorraine the organizer and Freddy the bus driver are staying at the motel. Margret's sister, Greta, also isn't here. She didn't come to dinner."

"Any idea where she might be?" Jason pulled out his notepad. "Or why she wasn't here for dinner?"

"She and Margret had a squabble over their rooms." Suzie grimaced. "They didn't seem to get along too well. Greta said she wouldn't be attending the dinner, and then didn't show up."

"We can go look for her. Let's check her room first?" Mary glanced over at Suzie.

"Okay." Jason followed Suzie and Mary toward Greta's room. Jason knocked, but there was no answer, so he knocked again.

"She must be out." Mary looked at her watch. "But it's dark already. Where do you think she would be?"

"Maybe she's out the back with Pilot." Suzie glanced toward the back door. "She was very eager to play with him."

"I guess it's possible. We have all of the lights on out there, and she wouldn't have been able to see all of the comings and goings from there." Mary nodded. "I noticed her heading toward the beach not long before dinner, so maybe she went to see Pilot on the way back. I haven't noticed her coming back to Dune House."

"All right. I'll send an officer with you." Jason pulled his radio from its holster.

"Wait, Jason." Mary met his eyes. "It might be better if it's just the two of us. It might be overwhelming if she sees an officer walking up to her. I know that at the moment everyone is a possible suspect, but she did just lose her sister. Even if they didn't get along, they're still family."

"Still family, yes." Jason tucked his radio back into its holster. "But someone might have made sure that Margret didn't make it to another birthday. You need to take that seriously. If this was deliberate, whoever did this is facing a murder charge, and they might be desperate to escape."

"We hear you." Mary took a deep breath. "We'll be careful. But we'll just be out the back."

CHAPTER 5

"I just can't believe this." Suzie wrung her hands as she walked down the back porch steps with Mary behind her. "How could she be fine one moment and dead the next? How could we not notice that anything was wrong?"

"If Summer is right, the poison was hidden in her food, and only her food. How could we know?" Mary took Suzie's hand for a moment and squeezed it before releasing it.

"There she is." Suzie started toward the yard with determined strides.

"It doesn't look like she's trying to hide." Mary grabbed Suzie's elbow to stop her. "Suzie, wait a second. What are you going to tell her?"

"What do you mean?" Suzie glanced over at her friend. "I'm going to tell her that Margret is dead."

"Just remember, it's her sister." Mary met her eyes. "It's going to be quite a shock."

"You're right." The sound of the waves crashing into the shore added to the chaotic noise of Suzie's thoughts. She had been so focused on locating Greta and trying to find out if she was involved in her sister's murder, that she'd lost sight of the fact that she might just be an innocent person whose sister had just died.

Mary watched as Greta threw a ball and Pilot eagerly raced after it.

"Are the festivities over already?" Greta smirked as they opened the gate and walked inside. "Did I miss all of the cake?"

Pilot ran over and dropped the ball at their feet. Greta patted his head.

"Greta." Mary offered her hand to her. "We need to tell you some terrible news."

"Terrible news?" Greta looked from one strained expression to the other, then shook her head. "It can't be that bad. What is it?"

"It's your sister." Suzie stroked the top of Pilot's head as he attempted to nuzzle her hand. "I'm afraid, she's passed away."

"You're afraid she has?" Greta raised her eyebrows and gave a short laugh. "That's nothing to be scared of, is it? Who killed her?"

Suzie glanced away to try to hide the shock that sparked through her at Greta's lighthearted reaction. One glaring truth stood out among Greta's response. She hadn't asked how did she die, she'd asked who killed her.

"At this time, we don't know what happened. The police are investigating, and I think it's very important that you speak with them. Will you come inside?" Suzie looked at Greta. Despite her flippant attitude, tears glistened in her blue eyes.

"Yes, of course I will." Greta looked toward the house. "I didn't realize anything had happened. I was on the beach before I came back here."

"I'm so very sorry for your loss," Mary said.

"My loss?" Greta mumbled as she patted Pilot's head. "I wish that I could see it that way."

Suzie and Mary exchanged a worried look.

Mary opened the gate, and Pilot darted ahead of them toward the house. She called him back to her side. She didn't want another incident.

"Do you know if anyone had been threatening Margret lately?" Suzie cast a sidelong glance in her direction and noticed a tear slither down her cheek.

"Lately?" Greta blinked, then shook her head. "It never stopped. The threats. The stalking. The lawsuits."

Suzie looked in the direction of the house and saw Beryl walking down the porch steps.

"Oh, Greta," Beryl called out. "I came to see if I could find you. I guess you've heard. I'm so sorry for your loss."

"It wasn't a great loss. We both know that." Greta continued toward the house. Beryl slipped between Mary and Greta. "How was she killed?"

"From what I overheard, and from the questions, they're going to do some tests, but they believe she may have been poisoned." Beryl cringed.

Mary knew Jason didn't want Greta told that the death might have been a murder, a poisoning, before he had a chance to speak to her, but it was too late now. "We did everything we could to save her."

"Poisoned?" A wistful smile crossed Greta's lips. "Of all the ways I imagined it, poisoning was never one of them."

"You imagined your sister being killed?" Mary's voice wavered in shock.

"Oh, I know, you're judging me. But you haven't lived my life. I've known for decades that Margret would die at someone else's hand. Everywhere she went, she left enemies in her wake, some that decided I was as good a target as she was, until they figured out that Margret didn't care what happened to me. I always knew she would be killed. It was just a matter of how and when." Greta glanced over her shoulder at the two of them. "Now, I'll have those answers."

"Was there anyone in particular that had ramped up their threats lately?" Suzie caught her arm. "Greta, was there anyone on this trip that had something against your sister?"

"I won't point any fingers." Greta pulled away and ascended the steps.

"Greta." Mary followed after her. "If someone did this to Margret, we can't be sure that they won't hurt anyone else. If you suspect someone, it's really important that you say so. If not to us than to the police, so that they can make sure that everyone stays safe."

"Is it?" Greta paused at the top of the steps and turned back to look at them. "My sister isn't my responsibility. I had to learn that a long time ago. I wasn't responsible for her life choices when she was alive, and I'm certainly not now that she's dead. I want nothing to do with her, or what happened to her. The way I see it, the safest thing I can do is stay out of it. So, whether it's you, or the police, I have nothing to say about any of it." She continued on toward the sliding glass door just as Jason stepped out through it.

"Greta?" Jason met her eyes. "I'm Detective Jason Allen. I'm so sorry for your loss."

"Please, don't bother to be." Greta pushed her way past him, through the door. "I'll be in my room!"

"Greta, if you could just give me a few minutes. I'm sure that you knew your sister best." Jason took a step toward her.

Greta spun around to face him. She glared straight into his eyes.

"Unless I'm under arrest, I'm leaving. I have nothing to say." She turned on her heel and continued through the house, toward the back hallway that led to her room. Beryl followed right behind her. "I need to be alone, Beryl." She glanced over her shoulder. Beryl stopped and turned back toward Suzie and Mary.

"I think she just needs some space, Beryl. People grieve differently, and she's clearly not ready to talk," Suzie said.

"You're right." Beryl walked away from them.

"The way she's acting, I'm not sure that she'll ever be ready to talk." Mary looked over at Suzie and Jason. "I can't imagine feeling that way about a family member dying. She seemed willing to talk to the police before, then she just changed her mind."

"Maybe that should tell us something." Suzie frowned. "Everyone was certainly shocked by Margret's passing, but no one seems heartbroken. If she could be so disliked in life, maybe there's a good reason."

"Maybe." Mary sighed.

"So far, everyone I've spoken to has had nothing pleasant to say about Margret. From what I've gathered, she crossed quite a few people, just in this small group." Jason glanced over his shoulder toward the living room. "I have my work cut out for me investigating this one. I think it would be easiest if everyone still stayed here for the night. Are you two okay with that?"

"Sure." Suzie scanned the faces in the living room. "We'll do our best to make them feel comfortable."

"Great, thanks Suzie. I know these are strange circumstances." Jason gestured to the kitchen. "In case this is a poisoning, my officers will take samples, and then everything will need to be thrown away. The whole kitchen and dining room will need to be thoroughly cleaned." He turned back to the living room and stepped inside with Mary just behind him. "I'll arrange it all for you."

Suzie started to follow after them, but a sharp tone from the kitchen stopped her.

"A woman has been murdered, poisoned, and you are the one responsible for providing the food that she ingested!"

CHAPTER 6

*S*uzie walked up to the kitchen doorway and spotted a young woman in a police uniform. She had Tasha cornered against the kitchen counter.

Suzie recognized the police officer. Jason had introduced her to Suzie as Officer Beth Chambers when they had crossed paths in town, but she was new to the area, and Suzie hadn't really spoken to her.

The officer's tone grew more shrill as she continued.

"I want to know exactly what you prepared, how you prepared it, and where it was prepared!"

Tasha burst into tears as she attempted to answer.

"I had nothing to do with this! Nothing. I didn't do anything wrong."

"Then why is someone dead, Tasha?" Beth's tone grew colder and sharper. "Can you explain that to me? People don't normally just drop dead on their birthday cake."

"Excuse me." Suzie stepped into the kitchen and slid her arm around Tasha's shoulders. "Tasha, it's all right. Just relax."

"I'm in the middle of gathering evidence." Beth's hard brown eyes locked on Suzie's. "Please don't interrupt."

"I absolutely will interrupt. What kind of evidence do you think you're going to collect when she can't even talk because she's so upset? You don't even know for sure if Margret was poisoned, yet." Suzie glanced over at Katrina who hovered near the kitchen door. "It's all right, Katrina, we're going to figure out what happened here."

Tension poured off the officer as she leaned closer to Suzie.

"I won't stand for interference in my investigation! As far as I'm concerned, this woman died under your roof, on your watch!"

"Beth!" Jason stepped into the kitchen, his voice stern and his gaze sharp. "I just asked you to find out where the food was prepared. What's happening here?"

Tasha sniffled as she pulled away from Suzie. "I prepared just about everything in my kitchen as I always do. Some of the sauces we prepared here right before dinner, and we cooked some of the food and baked the bread rolls here. But Jason, I swear, I had nothing to do with this."

"No one is accusing you, Tasha," Jason said.

"I beg to differ." Suzie looked at Beth. "Your officer was absolutely accusing her."

"I don't know how you were able to notice when you were so busy interfering with my investigation." Beth glared at Suzie.

"We all need to take a beat here." Jason took a step toward Beth. "Let's not lose focus on what matters here."

"You're right." Tasha took a deep breath. "I understand why you need to ask these questions. It's just overwhelming for me to think that something I served to Margret might have been poisoned. It breaks my heart. I know for certain I had nothing to do with it, but that doesn't change the fact that it happened. I will do anything I can to help the investigation."

"Thank you." Jason rested his hand on his belt

and looked into her eyes. "I appreciate your cooperation. If you don't mind, I'd like to take your statement. If you can walk me through your day, and your process for preparing the food, it would help a lot."

"Absolutely, I can do that." Tasha glanced over at Katrina. "Anything I don't remember, I'm sure that Katrina can help fill in."

"Yes." Katrina still hovered near the back door.

"Great." Jason shifted his attention to Beth. "You can go."

"I'll check in on the other guests that are giving their statements." Beth took a step toward the doorway.

"No, you can go." Jason's voice took on a harder tone. "Back to the station."

"Seriously?" Beth looked over her shoulder at him.

"We'll discuss this later." Jason focused on Tasha. "Let's step outside to talk."

Beth strode out through the back door without another word.

Suzie walked back toward the living room. A few officers continued to take statements from the guests. She looked around the room in search of Jason's partner, Detective Kirk Rondella, then she remembered that he was visiting his family for a few days over Thanksgiving. She spotted Mary seated right next to Vera, with her hand cradled in her own.

Vera stared, dazed, across the room while an officer attempted to question her.

"How is everyone holding up?" Suzie sat down beside Mary and kept her voice low.

"I think everyone is just eager to get out of the house. I've made some recommendations of restaurants, and shops to visit, tomorrow. And suggested they explore the beach. I know that it might be the last thing they're thinking about right now, but a little distraction might help them. I think it's going to take some time for everyone to really process what happened."

"I think so, too." Suzie wiped her hands across her face and sighed. "I'm going to need some time, too."

"Mary?" Detective Wes Brown's voice carried from the front door of the house.

"In here, Wes." Mary stood up and gently squeezed Vera's hand before releasing it.

Suzie slid over into Mary's place on the couch and picked up Vera's hand.

"Ma'am, were you and Margret good friends?"

The officer who questioned her leaned closer. "I just need to know if you knew her very well."

"No," Vera muttered the word. "Not well. Can I go, now?"

"Sure." The officer sat back and briefly met Suzie's eyes.

"Vera, do you want me to sit on the porch with you?" Suzie stood up as Vera did. "I can show you around. Lend a listening ear."

"No. I don't need your help." Vera refused to look at her as she stepped around her. "I want to be alone."

"Please let me know if you need anything." Suzie watched her go. Her mind spun with all of the possibilities of what might happen next. Any one of the people she'd welcomed as guests earlier in the day could be responsible for Margret's death. But they weren't the only people under suspicion. If Jason hadn't known Suzie and Mary so well, she guessed they would have been at the top of his list of suspects. She cringed at the thought of the rumors already spreading through town.

"What's happened?" a shrill voice broke through the murmuring of the police officers questioning the guests. Lorraine burst into the living room, her eyes wide, and her clipboard clutched in her hand.

"Margret's dead." John stood up from the chair he had been sitting in. "Poisoned, they say." He tipped his head toward Suzie.

"What?" Lorraine grabbed on to the back of the couch and gasped. "Please tell me this is some kind of prank."

"I'm afraid it isn't." Suzie walked over to her. "They still need to confirm it but they think she might have been poisoned. They are taking precautions at the moment in case she was." In all the chaos, Suzie hadn't thought to contact Lorraine to tell her what was happening.

"How did this happen?" Lorraine glared at her. "I trusted you! All of your reviews were wonderful!"

"Lorraine, it's not her fault." John walked over to her. "We don't know who did it yet, but I'm sure that Suzie and Mary had nothing to do with it."

Every set of eyes in the room swung toward Suzie. Her heart raced as she recognized the uncertainty in their eyes. Maybe Jason didn't suspect her, but these people didn't know her from anyone else. They had no reason to think that she didn't lace Margret's food with poison.

"Listen everyone, you're all still welcome to stay here tonight. If you need anything at all, please let me know." Suzie forced a smile to her lips, then wondered if that made her look even guiltier. She turned her focus on Lorraine. "If you'd like to step into the other room with me, I'll tell you everything I know so far."

"Yes." Lorraine stepped back out into the hall.

Suzie followed behind her. She could still feel the eyes of the guests on her.

CHAPTER 7

*S*uzie led Lorraine past the dining room toward the porch. She glanced at the dining room table as she walked past. The chairs were pushed back in a haphazard pattern. Memories of the moment when everyone realized something bad had happened, flashed through her mind. Suddenly she stopped and closed her eyes.

Suzie tried to stay within the memories that flooded her. What had everyone else at the table been doing? How had they reacted? Was there a clue in the way that they behaved? She recalled Vera's comments, and a few shocked looks, then her mind focused on Margret and trying to help her. No matter how hard she tried, she couldn't remember exactly how everyone had responded.

"Suzie, are you okay?" Lorraine asked.

"I'm sorry." Suzie opened her eyes. "I just got lost in my thoughts." She slid the door open to the porch and caught sight of Wes, Mary and Pilot just outside the door. "I'm very sorry for your loss, Lorraine." She closed the door behind her. "I know this is shocking. I have no idea how it could have happened. I can assure you that if there was foul play involved, the police will find out who is responsible and arrest that person."

"Can you?" Lorraine squinted at Suzie as she hugged her clipboard against her chest. "Because I recall you assuring me that my residents would have a great time at your B&B. I recall you assuring me that the area was safe and a pleasant place to visit. Obviously, that didn't turn out to be true."

"This really is a very safe area." Wes stepped away from Mary and closer to Suzie. "And these two do a fantastic job of running their B&B. Unfortunately, sometimes things are out of our control."

"I guess you're right." Lorraine sighed. "I'm just looking for someone to blame, when really I'm the one to blame. I never should have left them alone here. They had insisted that they didn't want supervision, that's why they wanted us to stay at the motel, and after that bus ride, I really needed a break from all of the bickering. But it was my responsibility to make sure that they were all safe, and I should have been here."

"Even if you had been here, there's nothing you could have done." Mary stepped up behind her and patted her shoulder. "Suzie was right there, ready to render aid, but it all happened so fast that nothing could be done to save her. All we can do now is try to get to the truth about what happened."

"It would probably be a good idea to speak to the police." Wes tipped his head toward Jason, who spoke with the caterers on another section of the porch. "Any information you can give them will help with the investigation."

"Okay, at least that's something I can do that might make a difference." Lorraine sniffled as she walked toward Jason.

"Thanks for helping, Wes." Mary wrapped her arms around his waist. "I'm glad you're here."

"Sorry it took me so long to get here." Wes pulled off his hat. "I heard about what happened, but I was following a lead on an old case that took me a few towns over. It's certainly been an eventful day for both of you."

"That's for sure." Suzie smiled as Pilot nudged

her hand. "He always has a way of showing up when we need him."

"That's a good boy." Wes patted the top of the dog's head, then looked up at Mary. "If you're not too tired, would you like to take a walk with me?"

"I'd like nothing better." Mary took his hand.

"There's a beautiful moon out tonight." Wes looked toward the sky.

"It is." Mary glanced over at Suzie. "You don't mind, do you? I know we're not quite done cleaning up."

"Not at all." Suzie rubbed Pilot's head.

"We'll take Pilot with. He could use a walk." Mary glanced down at the dog.

"Be careful." Suzie locked her eyes to Mary's. "We don't know exactly what happened here, yet, but we do suspect that Margret was poisoned. If that's the case, someone was close enough to Margret to commit murder. Whoever that person is might still be nearby."

"With my two boys with me, I couldn't be safer." Mary looked from Wes to Pilot. "Are you sure you want to stay here? You could walk with us."

"No, thanks." Suzie glanced over at Jason as he began interviewing Lorraine. "Hopefully, Jason will give me an update on what he thinks when he's finished his interviews." She pointed toward the path that led to the beach. "Go on, try to get away from all of this for a few minutes."

Suzie made her way toward Jason just in time to overhear his conversation with Lorraine.

"I'm not saying that she deserved to die, I'm just saying that she was not well liked. She forced her way into Shady Village. I still don't know exactly how. Her sister, Greta, had moved in a few years ago, and our residences were all full. But Margret made some kind of deal with the manager and was able to get a home that had already been promised to someone else. All of the residents knew about it and were not pleased that she had gamed the system. Rumors had been flying around that she had somehow forced the manager into it." Lorraine sighed. "I don't know if any of that is true, though. There's always some kind of scandal going on, and half of them turn out not to be true. I'm sorry, I wish I could be more helpful."

"This is very helpful, actually. Thank you." Jason looked up from his notebook. "Can you tell me anything about where she lived before she moved to Shady Village? I ran her name through the system, and it turned up dozens of addresses. I'm not sure which one was the most recent."

"I honestly have no idea. I hadn't met her before she moved in a few months ago. She just turned up. Apparently, Greta didn't know where she had been, for years. She wasn't part of her life. From the stories she told, she's lived all over. When we were driving into town, she did mention that she used to live in the area, in the neighboring town. But she said it was a long time ago. I can check with the manager to see if she has any information that I don't know about."

"That would be great, thanks." Jason offered her his card. "Feel free to reach out at any time."

"I will."

"You're welcome to stay as well, Lorraine, if you'd be more comfortable doing that," Suzie said as Lorraine turned toward her.

"No, but thank you, I have a room at the motel. The driver, Freddy, is staying there, too. It's a decent place. The residents pay for the trip, and they wanted the motel for us, because it is the cheaper option. They didn't want us staying with them. I know it sounds terrible after I said I should have been here when this all happened, but I really need some time to myself to go through all of this. If I stay at the B&B, the residents won't stop bothering me." Lorraine pursed her lips, then blew air through them. "I'd better go in and talk to the residents." She turned and walked back toward the house.

"What are you thinking, Jason?" Suzie asked. "Do you suspect that someone staying at Dune House poisoned Margret?"

"I suspect that my biggest problem with this investigation is going to be finding someone who didn't have something against her."

CHAPTER 8

The soothing sound of the waves crashing against the sand helped ease the tension in Mary's muscles, but it was the warmth of Wes' hand wrapped around hers that allowed her to take a deep breath and begin to process what had happened.

"How much does someone have to hate another person to poison them at their birthday dinner?" Mary looked over at Wes. "It's so hard for me to believe that someone was able to poison Margret right under our noses. I hope that Summer's wrong and Margret just died from natural causes."

"I can understand why you're hoping for that. I know it's difficult to believe she could be poisoned right under your nose, but poison is often colorless and odorless. Presuming this was a poisoning, whoever did it likely thought it would be assumed that Margret had a heart attack, or some other kind of medical incident. If Margret hadn't reacted the way she had before she died, and people hadn't been able to describe that reaction in so much detail, Summer might not have been able to detect the signs of a possible poisoning, and it wouldn't have been investigated."

"I just wish I did something different, so this could have been prevented. I offered to make the dinner, but they wanted to use a caterer instead." Mary squeezed his hand. "I was relieved, because they were so demanding, and it would have been a lot of work, but maybe if I had insisted. Maybe if I had made the meal instead, I would have been watching more closely. Maybe I would have noticed someone slipping something into the food."

"We don't even know if that is how she was poisoned. It's likely, but it's also possible it was in something that she drank, or even lipstick that she applied. We don't even know if she was poisoned for sure." Wes glanced over at her. "Right now, the best way we can use our energy is to eliminate suspects. There are so many, which makes it quite a task to narrow them down. Was there anyone you noticed that acted a little suspicious?"

"They were only here for a few hours before we had dinner. Between showing them their rooms and getting everything they needed, I honestly didn't even speak to many of them for very long." Mary closed her eyes for a moment, then shook her head. "I didn't notice anyone acting particularly strange. They were all a little out of sorts from the rough bus ride." She leaned against his arm and shivered as a cool breeze blew off the water.

"A bit chilly tonight."

"It is." Mary turned toward the water and took a deep breath of the salty air. "It's hard to believe that Suzie and I were just making plans for Thanksgiving, and now we're snooping around a possible murder that took place in our dining room."

A sharp bark from Pilot drew their attention. He dug at the sand with his paws and sniffed something beside the pile of sand by some rocks.

"What do you have there, buddy?" Wes squinted where Pilot dug.

"Drop it, Pilot!" Mary gave his leash a light tug as she did her best to crouch down beside him. "Remember what happened the last time you got too friendly with a crab?"

Pilot whimpered and backed up a few steps.

"It's some kind of paper." Mary pointed the flashlight on her phone at it. "It must have got caught between the rocks, which kept it from blowing away." She plucked the paper out from between the rocks. "Who would be careless enough to just toss litter onto the beach?" She gasped as she caught sight of the letterhead on the paper. "Oh dear, it's a piece of stationery from Dune House. I wonder how it got out here?"

"What's that written on it?" Wes turned on the flashlight on his phone and pointed it at the paper.

"It's part of a note. Some of the paper has been torn." Mary squinted at the words, then looked up at Wes with wide eyes. "It mentions Margret!"

"Read it to me." Wes continued to train the beam of his flashlight on the paper.

"Some of the words are missing. It says 'because of your behavior, Margret,' and then it's ripped, but underneath that, it says, 'you can never be forgiven,' and under that, it says, 'you'll pay for what you did.'" Mary's hand trembled as she held the paper out to Wes. "I think it's possible that Margret's killer wrote this note."

"We need to get it examined right away." Wes pulled a pack of tissues from his pocket and handed her one. "Try to hold it just by the corner. With it being out here in the elements, there probably isn't much chance of finding evidence on it, but we should still be careful."

"Okay, yes, I'll be careful." Mary clutched the note with the tissue and looked back toward the house. "I think this proves one thing, Wes."

"What's that?" Wes took Pilot's leash from her and encouraged the dog to walk back toward the house.

"If the killer did write this note, then whoever killed Margret is a guest at Dune House." Mary took another deep breath of the salty air and felt it pump through her veins. "We may have just narrowed things down enough to give us a place to start."

"That may be true, but first we have to prove that the person who wrote the note is the same person that killed Margret. It's pretty clear that many people here have things against her. Maybe the note is just a nasty note." Wes shrugged. "It would be quite a coincidence, but without further proof, it doesn't mean too much."

"It means that someone staying at Dune House was angry enough to write it." Mary glanced over at him as they started back toward the house. "But I wonder if Margret ever received it? How did it end up out here?" She looked over her shoulder at the ocean. "It's breezy enough to have blown out onto the beach, but still, the paper would have had to be somewhere that the wind could catch it."

"Maybe Margret received it and took it out onto the beach to read it?" Wes paused at the bottom of the stairs that led up to the porch.

"When she arrived today, she had to use a cane and the ramp to get into the house. I'm not sure that she would venture out onto the beach on her own. It didn't appear that she would be able to handle navigating the sand. But it's possible, I guess." Mary waved to Suzie as she walked around a corner of the house and waved to them from the porch. "Suzie! We've found something!"

CHAPTER 9

Suzie met Mary and Wes at the top of the steps. "What did you find?" Her eyes widened as Mary held the note out to her.

"We found it caught between some rocks on the beach. Actually, Pilot did." Mary gave the dog a light pat on his back. "It's torn, but it's pretty clear that the note was written to Margret."

"And the author doesn't hold back about how they feel about Margret." Wes waved to a man who walked across the porch toward them. "Paul, it's good you're here."

"Not soon enough, I'm afraid." Paul opened his arms to Suzie for a hug.

"I'm just glad you were coming back today and you're not still out in the middle of the ocean." Suzie hugged him, then pulled away and looked back at Mary and Wes. "We need to figure out who wrote that note."

"But how?" Mary paused as Suzie filled Paul in on what was found. "No one signed it, or if they did, it's on the missing pieces."

"Well, there's one way to try to find out." Suzie glanced toward the sliding glass door that led into the house. "We take the notepads that have had paper used from them and use them ourselves and put new ones, along with envelopes, in each room before new guests arrive. If we take a look at the notepads in each room when we tidy up, we might be able to tell which one has been used."

"Yes, I suppose so." Mary glanced at the door as well. "We'll have to wait until morning to clean their rooms, like we normally do."

"At least if we check, we might be able to narrow down who might have written the note," Suzie said.

"I'll set up breakfast out on the porch, and that should keep everyone busy long enough for you to do all of the rooms."

"Good idea." Suzie glanced at her watch. "I think we should all get some rest. It's been a long day."

"I agree." Mary shooed Pilot toward the door. "I'll make sure he stays put in my room."

"Mind if I stay for a few minutes?" Wes followed her to the door.

"Of course." Mary slid open the door and stepped inside with Wes behind her.

As the door slid shut behind them, Paul took a step away from Suzie. "I guess I should head back to the boat."

"I'll walk with you." Suzie slipped her hand into his.

"I thought you were tired?"

"I am, but I'd love to talk this out with you. If you wouldn't mind?" Suzie raised her eyebrows. "You have a knack for helping me figure things out."

"Do I?" Paul smiled as he ran his thumb along the back of her hand. "Then, absolutely, please walk with me." He led her around the house to the front porch, and down the steps into the parking lot. "I wish I had been here earlier. I know you handle everything so well, Suzie, but I wish I was here."

"So do I." Suzie looked up at the stars sprinkled across the sky. "It's certainly not how I expected this visit to go. But there's no way to change it. Now, all I want to do is help to try to find out what really happened. To find out who killed her. But, Paul, I have absolutely no clue who did this to Margret. I keep running the whole day through my mind, waiting for something to pop out as suspicious. But there's nothing. The group didn't get along with Margret, but that's normal, isn't it. I can't see any of them murdering her. The two people that stood out to me the most were Margret, and her sister. They fought over the rooms that were available to them. They were so mean to each other that I thought they would ruin the trip with their attitudes." She continued across the street toward the dock.

"Then you did notice something. It did stand out to you. Margret's sister might have decided to get rid of her." Paul winced. "I know that it sounds horrible, but it's possible."

"I have thought about that, but Greta, Margret's sister, was the only person staying at Dune House who wasn't at the dinner. How could she slip poison into Margret's food, if she wasn't there?" Suzie stepped onto the wooden planks of the dock. The cool breeze that carried off the water inspired subtle creaks and sloshes from the boats in the slips.

"That she wasn't there for her own sister's birthday celebration makes me even more suspicious." Paul narrowed his eyes. "Maybe she thought if she wasn't present she wouldn't be a suspect, she wouldn't be blamed. Maybe she found a way to do it before she left, or maybe she joined forces with someone else to do it?" He held up his hands. "I'm just playing devil's advocate here. I trust your instincts completely, and if you felt something was off from the beginning between these two sisters, then I don't doubt that there is something to be found. Don't question your instincts."

"It just feels wrong to accuse someone who has just lost her sister." Suzie looked over the water, then turned back to Paul. "It's hard to believe that someone could harbor that much hatred."

"Siblings don't always automatically bond. In fact, sometimes, they can be downright cruel to each other. Now that we know someone in Dune House wrote a note like that to Margret, it's pretty clear that someone definitely hated Margret, and wished her harm." Paul brushed her hair back from her cheek and looked into her eyes. "I'm not sure I like the idea of you going back to that house and sleeping under the same roof as a murderer."

"The one thing that note does indicate was that Margret was targeted. This wasn't a random killing. That makes me feel more confident that no one else in the house will be hurt." Suzie cupped his cheeks and smiled. "I'll be fine. I promise."

"I'm holding you to that." Paul gave her a soft kiss.

Suzie glanced over her shoulder at Dune House. As its windows glowed from the hill it perched on, and the moonlight streamed down across its rich paint and historic architecture, it was hard for her to believe that such a beautiful place could be the scene of a murder only hours earlier.

CHAPTER 10

he sound of the front door closing startled Suzie awake the next morning. She'd passed out as soon as her head hit the pillow, and even as she forced her eyes open, the desire to sleep continued to cling to her. She wiped at her eyes and took a deep breath. Immediately, things felt off. Normally, she'd be greeted by the delicious aroma of fresh coffee brewing. As an early riser, Mary always had a pot going by the time Suzie woke up, and usually had whipped up some eggs and toast for them to share for breakfast.

No aromas filled the air, only the faint scent of salt from the ocean. She sat up, instantly concerned about Mary. Then it struck her. No coffee could be made in a house where someone had been poisoned.

No food could be cooked. Not until it was deemed safe.

Suzie quickly got dressed. Once she felt like she looked presentable, she went downstairs. As she walked into the living room, she found Mary just stepping into it with a few boxes and a drink holder.

"Oh, let me help you!" Suzie grabbed the drink carrier and set it down on one of the tables in the living room, where there were already a couple and some boxes.

"I woke up early this morning to start preparing breakfast and then realized that I couldn't serve the guests anything from our kitchen." Mary set the boxes down on the table. "So, I raided the bakery for everything that I thought they might like." She shook out her arms as she laughed. "I didn't think through how I would get it all in and out of the car, though!"

"You should have woken me. I would have gone with you." Suzie breathed in the aroma of the fresh coffee and began relaxing.

"Honestly, I don't think I would have been able to say a word to you. I was in desperate need of coffee this morning. I didn't get much sleep last night." Mary looked over the drinks and food. "But if you'd like to help me get this set up, I won't turn that down."

"Sure, of course." As Suzie reached for a box, her phone beeped with a text. "It's from Jason." Suzie read it, then looked up at Mary. "Tests show that she definitely was poisoned. But they don't know how, yet."

"Wow. I knew it was likely, but I hoped Summer was wrong and Margret died of natural causes."

"I know. Now we need to work out who did this." Suzie piled up a few boxes and headed out through the sliding doors. "I thought I wouldn't sleep last night, but I actually zonked out the moment my head hit the pillow." She set the boxes on the large table on the wraparound porch. "I slept soundly. I guess I was more exhausted than I realized."

"I'm sure you were." Mary set a drink carrier down on the table. "I just couldn't stop thinking about what happened to Margret and that note. I hope that they're able to figure out who wrote it."

"Me, too." Suzie glanced up as John stepped out through the door.

"Is that coffee I smell?" John smiled.

"Yes, and donuts and pastries and bagels." Mary began opening one of the boxes.

"Wow, you'd think you were feeding an army." John chuckled.

"Breakfast?" Vera poked her head out through the door. "Count me in. I'm starving!"

"How can any of you even think about eating?" Greta's voice carried from a nearby chair, causing Suzie and Mary to jump with surprise. "After watching my sister die from poisoned food?" She stood up from the chair and walked over to the table. "I don't think I'll ever be able to eat again!"

"I bought all of this from a local bakery. None of it was prepared in the kitchen." Mary clasped her hands together. "But I can understand why you would be hesitant."

"Relax, I'm just kidding." Greta grinned as she grabbed a donut from the box. "I hope you got some cream cheese for those bagels."

"Absolutely, and lots of other spreads." Mary began opening more boxes.

Once all of the guests had filtered out onto the porch to eat, Suzie excused herself. She started down the hallway in the direction of the guest rooms to clean and tidy them. She hoped that she could work out who might have written the note.

Suzie stopped in John's room first. Everything appeared neat as a pin. His packed suitcase sat on one side of the bed, while the blankets and sheets were pulled back from the other side. Suzie found it a little strange that he slept with his suitcase, and that he hadn't unpacked. But she knew everyone had their quirks, and considering the events of the night before, she guessed that some people would be acting a little strange.

Suzie walked over to the desk and looked at the stationery holder. The notepads, envelopes, and pens all looked untouched. She tidied the bed and replaced the towels, then gave the room a quick vacuum. She took one more look around the room, then stepped out and pulled the door shut behind her.

As Suzie opened the door to the next room, she realized it belonged to Greta. She recalled Paul's advice to trust her instincts. She pushed the door open and took a sharp breath.

"Someone has already been in here." Suzie froze in the doorway. She swept her gaze around the ransacked room. Every drawer had been pulled out and emptied. The sheets and blankets were torn off the bed and tossed into a pile on the floor. Even the pillowcases had been removed and strewn about the room.

"What's happened here?" Greta gasped from just behind her. "What have you done?"

"It wasn't me." Suzie spun around to face her. "I just found it like this. How long have you been out of your room this morning?"

"About an hour. I took a walk along the beach when I woke up, and I haven't been back in here since." Greta's voice trembled. "Why would someone do this? Margret is dead. Does this mean that someone is after me, too? I have to get out of this place!"

"Greta, I know this is very alarming." Suzie wrapped her arm around her shoulders. "I'll have the police come and investigate. I'll set you up in another room, where you'll be safe."

"Safe?" Greta laughed. "My sister was murdered at your dining room table! And now look at this! How exactly do you plan to keep me safe?"

"If you'd rather, I can pay for a room for you at the motel where Lorraine and Freddy are staying. It's the only other accommodation place in Garber," Suzie offered. "Whatever I can do to make this easier on you, just tell me."

"Not a chance. I don't want to be anywhere near that busybody and that grimy driver. You know which room I want." Greta crossed her arms as she looked into Suzie's eyes.

"I don't think I can do that, Greta. The police searched it, but I'm not sure they would be okay with someone staying in it." Suzie glanced toward the door across the hall.

"So, you're going to deny me my last chance to be close to my sister? Like you said, the police already searched it. All you need to do is let me stay there. Or is that too much trouble after everything that I've been through?" Greta put her hands on her hips.

"Of course not." Suzie bit into the tip of her tongue. She wanted to say a lot more. She wanted to point out that she was certain that the only reason she wanted to stay in Margret's room was because she had wanted to be in that room the entire time. Instead, she took a slow breath. "I'll make a call right now and confirm whether the police have released the room. If it has been released, then we'll get you moved right in."

"Thank you." Greta smiled. "Finally, some of the courtesy I envisaged while staying here. I want to know within the hour." She glanced back at the mess in her room. "And I'm sure you don't expect me to tidy this up?"

"Not at all. I'll make sure everything gets safely into your new room." Suzie forced a smile.

As Suzie watched Greta walk back down the hallway, she pulled her phone out of her pocket and dialed Jason's number.

"Busy at the moment, Suzie, is it urgent?"

"Maybe?" Suzie looked over the destroyed room. "It appears that someone broke into Greta's room in search of something. It would probably be best if you take a look. I can't guarantee that Greta didn't do it herself."

"Why would Greta do something like that?" Jason's voice raised with suspicion. "Yes, I'll head over now."

"I'm not sure, but she's determined to get into the room that Margret had been staying in. I told her I wasn't sure if that would be possible." Suzie paused and lowered her voice. "Is it?"

"Yes, it is. We have thoroughly searched the room and released it. But it does seem strange that she would want to stay in there."

"The two argued over the room before Margret died. She claims she just wants to move in there to be close to the memory of her sister, but my instincts tell me she just wants the room." Suzie sighed. "Maybe I'm just being judgmental and callous."

"Maybe not. I've never known you to be that way, Suzie. I'll be there soon. Don't let anyone else into Greta's room until I have a chance to look through it."

"Okay, I won't." Suzie ended the call, then locked the door to Greta's room.

CHAPTER 11

*S*uzie cleaned the rest of the rooms but didn't find anything suspicious or any indication that any of the notepads had been used.

Once she was finished, she headed out onto the porch.

All of the guests, including Greta, had gathered around the table and were enjoying their breakfast.

"Morning, all!" Lorraine walked up to them from the front of the house. "I didn't think adding the word good would be appropriate." She paused at the sight of the spread on the table. "That all looks so delicious. The breakfast they offered at the motel was cereal. This looks much better."

"There's plenty." Mary swept her hand over the table. "Please help yourself."

"Thank you." Lorraine settled into a chair beside Vera, then grabbed a bagel. "Have the police offered any update yet today?"

"I just spoke with Detective Allen. He's on his way here. He might have an update for you then." Suzie picked up one of the cups of coffee and started to take a sip. She hesitated as her mind flashed back to the way Margret had collapsed. She forced the thought away and sipped the coffee. If she wanted her guests to feel comfortable, she had to find a way to be comfortable, too.

"While the police are conducting the investigation, I thought you all might enjoy the local art exhibition that's on in town at the moment." Mary smiled as she looked up from her phone. "I just had them set aside a ticket for each of you. You can use it or not. It's up to you." She looked up at the sky. "It's supposed to be sunny and warmer than usual for fall today, so you might want to spend some time on the beach as well."

"They all sound like good options." John looked up from his bagel. "Whatever we can do to keep ourselves busy, right?"

"Right," Suzie agreed.

"I guess Freddy isn't gassing the bus up, yet?"

Vera looked over at Lorraine. "We're not heading back home, yet?"

"Not as long as the police would rather we stay. It's hard to imagine going back without Margret being along for the trip." Lorraine cringed.

"It'll be more peaceful, that's for sure." Chip grinned as he handed a buttered bagel over to Beryl.

"Don't talk like that, Chip." Beryl swatted his arm. "Margret may have been a pill, but she was still a person, and she didn't deserve to be murdered. Her sister is right there."

"Oh, don't hold back on my account. Margret got exactly what she deserved. I wish that wasn't the case, but trust me, whoever killed her did us all a favor." Greta smirked.

"Oh, Greta." Lorraine sighed and leaned over to take her hand. "You can put on that tough front all you want. I know that you're hurting."

"The only reason I'm hurting is because my vacation has been interrupted. I just wanted a few days away with my friends for a Thanksgiving celebration, like we do every year, and the next thing I know my sister has hijacked my trip and made it all about her birthday." Greta jerked her hand away. "She always ruined everything. As far as I'm concerned you need to tell Freddy to gas up that bus and have it ready to roar out of here the first moment we can." She snatched up another donut as she turned, then stalked off.

"Should someone go with her?" Vera stood up. "She probably shouldn't be alone at a time like this."

"I think she wants to be alone." Lorraine sipped her coffee and sat back in her chair. "It's going to take her time to process all of this."

"How is Freddy taking it, Lorraine?" Suzie asked. "I'm sure you told him."

"He isn't much of a talker, so I'm not sure. But I did tell him, and the police came to speak to him at the motel last night. But I haven't seen him out of his room since." Lorraine shrugged.

Suzie and Mary met eyes across the table.

Once the guests had dispersed and the table had been cleared, Mary picked up her purse.

"I'm guessing that we had the same thought?"

"Absolutely. It's time to talk to Freddy about what he might have noticed on the bus." Suzie grabbed her purse and keys and headed for the door. "I don't want to stay away from the B&B for too long, but I'm curious about what he might have observed during that long drive. If one of the guests poisoned Margret, they had to have the poison stashed somewhere. My guess is they might have been acting nervous, too."

"Let's find out."

"I didn't find any indication that any of the notepads had been used," Suzie said.

"That's weird."

"It is. Maybe I just couldn't tell." Suzie started down the porch steps. "I need to stop at the post office on the way."

"Okay."

"There's Jason, finally." Suzie watched as he walked toward them. "Jason, I almost forgot you were coming!"

"Sorry for the delay. I got caught up because a couple of people that knew Margret in the past returned my calls. Well, at least people that knew her, not necessarily as Margret."

"Are you saying she's had multiple names, Jason?" Mary raised her eyebrows.

"Both first and last. She's been married and divorced a few times, but from what I can tell, she's also had some fake identities, which is going to make all of this even harder. I asked the crime scene investigators to come out and go through Greta's room."

"I think everyone is out of the house right now,

so they shouldn't have any interruptions," Suzie said.

"Good, hopefully they'll uncover something." Jason looked over her purse and the keys clutched in her hand. "Where are you off to?"

"The post office, to post some Christmas gifts I've been meaning to send." Suzie glanced at Mary, then flashed a smile at Jason. She didn't want to tell him they were going to speak to Freddy. She imagined he wouldn't be happy about it. "I'll let you know if we hear anything else."

"Please do." Jason headed into the house.

CHAPTER 12

*A*fter stopping at the post office, Suzie parked in front of the motel and scanned the identical doors before her.

"I wonder which room is his."

Mary looked at the rooms.

"There!" She pointed at one of the rooms. "Room fourteen. I think I just saw him through the window. It can't hurt to knock, right?"

"Absolutely." Suzie followed her to the door.

Mary knocked hard three times.

The door jerked open at the same moment that a man's voice shouted through it.

"What is it?"

Mary took a step back. "Freddy, calm down!"

"Oh, sorry," Freddy stumbled over his words as

he looked over the two women. "I didn't expect it to be you two." He rubbed his hand through his hair. "I thought it might be the cops again."

"And that's how you would greet them? Why?" Mary asked.

"Why? Because they keep asking me questions I don't have answers to." Freddy sighed as he stepped back into the motel room. "Come on in. I'm sure you're going to do the same thing."

"We just want to see how you're holding up." Suzie stepped inside, and Freddy picked up a cup of coffee. "It's been quite a shock for all of us, and yes, we're trying to figure out what happened."

"It's tragic, for sure. But I have no idea what happened to her. I was here all night. I had nothing to do with the celebration dinner." Freddy had a sip. "All I wanted to do was crash. Now, I'm waiting to find out if we're going to be leaving today."

"I don't think you will be." Mary stepped farther into the motel room. "The police have asked all of the people involved in the trip to remain in the area while they conduct their investigation. Weren't you told that?"

"Oh, probably. Those cops had a lot to say. I just tuned them out after the first few sentences. But, hey, as long as we're staying, I'm still getting paid."

Freddy shrugged. "Seeing as I'm stuck here, maybe you can let me enjoy my solitude?"

"We'll do that." Suzie smiled. "We just want to know if you noticed anything strange on the bus ride. Did anyone sound particularly angry at Margret?"

"Are you kidding?" Freddy set his mug down on a table and laughed. "That woman tortured all of us for the whole ride. If she wasn't telling very embellished stories, she was singing, and it was even worse if she fell asleep, the snoring was ridiculous." He sighed. "I guess I shouldn't say that about someone that's died, but she really made the whole ride miserable. I heard people grumbling the whole time."

"What about Lorraine? She seems to be determined to do a good job. Did she say anything about how difficult Margret was being?" Mary swept her gaze around the messy room. A pile of dirty clothes on a chair, scattered beer bottles on every hard surface, the blankets torn off the bed, all of it made her wonder if he'd had some kind of party the night before.

"A few times. Once she said to me, how much would I have to pay you to pull over for a bathroom break and drive off without her?" Freddy chuckled.

"I told her I'd do it free of charge if she said the word. But we were just joking. I'm sure she never would have gone through with it. Now, can you leave me in peace? It's not often that I get a few paid days off."

"All right, yes, we'll be going." Suzie stepped out the door with Mary close behind her. They started back toward the car.

After a few steps, Suzie froze in her tracks as she looked at the ground.

"What is it?" Mary followed Suzie's line of sight as she picked up a notepad.

"It's from Dune House." Suzie turned it over in her hand.

"How did that get here?" Mary looked at the notepad.

"I don't know, but we need to see if we can find out." Suzie paged through it. "It has some pages missing."

"It has to be someone who was at Dune House that dropped it here, right?" Mary asked.

"Right," Suzie agreed.

"And it's still quite clean. It isn't wet from the rain yesterday, and it isn't covered by leaves or anything, so it was probably left here recently." Mary pointed at a camera in the corner of the overhang. "Let's see if we can find out who was here that had access to Dune House and dropped this pad of paper last night."

After a quick knock on the manager's office door, a man who looked to be in his forties with a thick mustache and a long beard appeared. Suzie recognized him as the owner, Pat. He had owned the motel for a while, but he tended to keep to himself.

"Need a room?" He looked between the two of them. "Don't I know you?"

"Probably. We own Dune House. Suzie and Mary." Suzie gestured to herself, then Mary.

"Oh, you two." Pat rolled his eyes. "All I hear is how nice that place is. It puts the pressure on me to dress things up around here."

"Sorry about that." Mary cleared her throat. "We need to have a look at your camera footage from last night, please."

"Oh?" Pat stared at them. "Am I just supposed to hand it over?" He laughed. "What are you two doing, playing detectives?"

"It's a simple request." Suzie tried to keep the frustration out of her voice. "I would assume that you've heard about the tragedy that took place at Dune House last night?"

"Sure. I guess you have some trouble keeping your guests alive." Pat crossed his arms as he smiled.

"It's nothing to joke about," Mary huffed.

"You're right, sorry." Pat blushed. "But what happened at Dune House has nothing to do with me or my motel. I have no reason to show you the footage."

"It could be important to the investigation." Suzie took a step toward him. "Please, it'll only take us a few minutes."

"If it's important to the investigation, then the police will come here to ask for it." Pat closed the door.

"I thought he might be a little more friendly." Suzie looked over at Mary. "I doubt Jason will be able to get a warrant for the footage based on a pad of stationery found on the ground. We may have hit a dead end."

"All he asked for was a police officer to make the request. Luckily, we know someone else with a badge." Mary smiled as she pulled out her phone and called Wes.

CHAPTER 13

"*A*re you sure he's going to be willing to help us?" Suzie watched Wes' car pull into the parking lot of the motel. "I doubt that Jason would."

"Wes is more flexible." Mary winked at her. "He's had more time on the job. He told me it wouldn't be a problem. Let's just see what he can do."

Wes stepped out of his car and walked over to them. "I'm here to be of service." He smiled at both of them.

"I don't think he's going to be easy to convince." Suzie glanced at the door to the manager's office. "He was pretty stubborn with us."

"Don't worry, I know Pat quite well. He'll help me out." Wes tipped his head toward the office door. "What I can't promise you is that the cameras were functional. Pat does his best to keep up with things, but sometimes, when things break, he can't always afford to fix them."

"Hopefully, the cameras were working last night." Mary walked toward the door of the office, with Suzie a few steps behind her.

Wes knocked on the door.

It swung open, followed by an annoyed growl.

"I told you no!"

"Pat." Wes stepped into the doorway.

"Wes." Pat took a step backward.

"I've told you about my girlfriend, Mary, right?" Wes gestured to Mary.

"This Mary?" Pat cleared his throat.

"This Mary." Wes nodded. "So, are you going to let us have a look at that footage or not?"

"Of course. For you, anything," Pat stumbled over his words as he stepped backward into the office. "I'm sorry. I didn't realize."

"It's all right, Pat." Wes patted him on the shoulder. "Just get last night's feed up, okay?"

"Sure thing." Pat hit a few keys on the keyboard,

then a video popped up on the screen. "This is the best I can do." He winced at the sight of the distorted footage.

"That's all right, it's something." Wes peered at the screen.

"Do you have anything that shows who entered and left the rooms?" Suzie asked.

"No." Pat put his hands in his pockets. "We only have one camera that covers some of the paths leading to the rooms. It's the best we've got at the moment."

"It's better than nothing." Wes leaned against the desk. "Any idea of the time we should be looking for, ladies?"

"After dark, at least," Mary said. "It was raining for a bit last night and the paper is dry."

"Okay, let's roll it forward." Wes tapped a key, then stopped as the footage shifted to the evening. "Looks like it was a pretty quiet night."

"Wait!" Suzie pointed to the screen. "Someone just walked down the path where the notepad was found. Roll it back."

"Just a second." Wes hit the key again. "Here we go. Good eye, Suzie."

"Who is that?" Mary squinted at the camera. "Can we make it any bigger?"

"I'm afraid not." Pat leaned forward and looked at the screen. "This cheap setup is all the budget allowed for."

"It definitely looks like a woman, right?" Suzie tilted her head to the side.

"I think so." Wes stared at the screen. "It's too bad there aren't cameras facing the parking lot. We might have been able to see which car belonged to her."

"Like I said, this is the best I could do." Pat shrugged. "Sorry I couldn't be of more help."

"You've been very helpful, Pat." Wes smiled. "Thanks for letting us have a look."

Suzie snapped a picture of the screen with her phone, then stood up. "At least we have a time stamp. We know when the woman arrived at the motel, and it was very late last night. Maybe we can figure out if one of the guests was missing from the house at that time."

"I was up most of the night, and I don't remember hearing anyone come or go." Mary followed Suzie to the door. "But remember, the guests weren't the only women at Dune House, yesterday."

"Do you mean Lorraine?" Suzie stepped out

through the door, then held it for Mary and Wes to step through.

"Yes, Lorraine, but also Tasha and Katrina. I hate to say it, but we can't rule them out. We gave Tasha one of the Dune House notepads when she was making notes for the dinner, so we could organize the timing and everything." Mary lowered her voice. "And Tasha and Katrina are the ones who made and served the food after all."

"You're right. We should at least talk to them." Suzie glanced at Wes. "Thank you for your help, Wes. He wasn't going to let us see the footage without you being here."

"Anything I can do to help." Wes waved to them, then walked over to his car.

As Suzie settled in her car and started it, her cell phone began ringing.

Mary picked up the phone and glanced at the screen. "It's Jason."

"Answer it, please." Suzie backed out of the parking space as Mary answered the phone.

"Hi, Jason, it's Mary. I'm going to put you on speaker." Mary set the phone down in the center console.

"I just wanted to let you both know we've finished processing Greta's room. Unfortunately, we didn't find anything that will point us in the direction of a particular suspect."

"You know Mary and Wes found that note on the beach last night." Suzie knew that Wes had given it to Jason. "Well, we just found some Dune House stationery on a path at the motel. The note was written on the same stationery. I'll send you a picture we got from the security camera footage, but it doesn't show much. It was of someone walking near where we found the notepad. We think it was a woman. I'm not sure where it might lead, but it's something."

"Wow!" Jason's voice raised. "You two have been sticking your noses in this. I shouldn't be surprised. And I know you won't stop no matter what I say. How did you manage to get to see the camera footage?"

"Wes helped." Suzie glanced over at Mary. "We knew it wouldn't be enough to get a warrant, but Wes is friends with the motel owner, Pat."

"It might be helpful later on. If it does happen to be related to Margret's death, it might help with a timeline. I did a deep dive into information about Margret and came across something interesting. Apparently, she lived in Parish about ten years ago. She didn't live there long, but from what I've been able to track down so far, she had some connections in Garber."

"Are you saying that you think it's possible someone in Garber might have killed her?" Suzie gripped the steering wheel tighter. "Someone we might know?"

"It's quite a stretch, but at the moment I can't rule it out. Several of the guests said they went and explored the town after arriving. From what I've been told, Margret stayed at Dune House, but I guess it's possible no one knew she went out. If she did, she could have run into some old friends, or enemies. I've asked Greta about it, but she insists she wasn't in contact with her sister during that time, and she has no idea who she might have known in the area." Jason paused. "I'm only telling you this because I know you are going to keep investigating, and you need to be cautious of everyone."

"Of course," Suzie said.

Jason ended the call.

"So, Margret had connections here?" Mary leaned back in her seat as Suzie turned into the parking lot of Tasha's Catering. "That certainly expands our suspect list."

"It does." Suzie parked the car, and they got out

and walked toward the door. Suzie took a deep breath as she grabbed the door handle, then looked over at Mary. "Are you ready for this? We have to keep an open mind that they could possibly be involved."

"I will do my best."

CHAPTER 14

*S*uzie opened the door and stepped inside Tasha's shop front.

"Oh, Suzie!" Tasha threw her arms around her before she could get fully through the door. "I'm so sorry! So very sorry!"

"Tasha, are you okay?" Suzie pulled away from her as she met her eyes. "Have you been crying?"

"Have I been crying?" Tasha sucked down a breath, then let out a wail. "Of course I've been crying! I haven't stopped crying all night!" She caught sight of Mary as she stepped inside. "Oh, Mary!" she wailed again and flung her arms around Mary's shoulders. "I'm so sorry!"

"It's okay, Tasha." Mary hugged her in return. "It's not your fault."

"Isn't it, though?" Tasha whimpered as fresh tears coursed down her cheeks. "I provided the food. How could it not be my fault?"

"Jason doesn't even know for sure how Margret was poisoned, yet." Suzie glanced around the shop, which displayed a variety of different party setups and catering menus. "He's going to do a thorough investigation, and I'm sure he'll get to the truth."

The door swung open, and Officer Beth Chambers stepped inside. She looked over Suzie and Mary, then settled her gaze on Tasha.

"May I speak with you for a few minutes?"

"Of course." Tasha walked over to her with a nervous smile. "I'm not sure what else I can tell you that I haven't already told you, though."

"I just need to go over a few things in your statement." Beth shot a stern look in Suzie and Mary's direction. "I'd rather speak with you alone."

"I don't mind if they stay. They might be able to help jog my memory on a few things." Tasha clasped her hands together.

"It's best if we speak in private." Beth crossed her arms.

"It's okay, we'll go." Suzie looked at Tasha. "Call us if you need anything, Tasha."

"Thank you, Suzie. I will." Tasha turned toward

Beth. "Why don't we speak in my office?" She led her toward a small room on the other side of the shop.

"Beth really has a problem with us, doesn't she?" Mary met Suzie's eyes.

"With me, in particular, I think." Suzie sighed. "I'm not looking forward to dealing with her in the future."

"I'm sure she's just young and eager. She'll calm down soon enough." Mary watched as Beth closed the door to the office behind her.

"Let's go out through the back." Suzie started down a hallway that led to the industrial kitchen.

"Suzie, we're supposed to leave." Mary followed after her.

"And we are, just not the way we came in." Suzie winked at her, then stepped into the kitchen. She froze at the sight of Katrina beside the trash can.

She tossed something into it, then spun around to face them.

"Oh! I didn't hear you come in." Katrina looked startled. She pulled her earbuds out and blushed. "I like to listen to music while I'm cleaning."

"Me, too." Mary smiled. "We're just on our way out." She tipped her head toward the door.

"This way?" Katrina stared at her. "Why didn't you go out the front?"

"There's an officer out there talking with Tasha. We just thought we'd see if you were here. We wanted to make sure that you are doing okay." Suzie searched her eyes. "You've been through a lot."

"That's true." Katrina clenched her hands into fists. "I still can't believe what happened. I can't believe that someone did this. The cops searched our kitchen top to bottom last night and wiped out everything we had in stock." She sighed. "It's going to take some time to clean everything, then once we get the all clear, we have to restock everything to get us operational again."

"I'm sorry to hear that." Suzie looked over the empty cabinets and cleared off counters. "They did the same at Dune House. I guess they have to be cautious."

"Of course." Katrina nodded.

"We're still trying to figure out who might have done it. Did you notice anything strange yesterday about any of the guests? Did anyone complain about their food, or ask for something extra?" Mary settled her gaze on Katrina.

"No, not at all. Everyone was very polite. That's the odd thing. I expected a little bit of consternation from that group, but no one complained about anything or sent anything back." Katrina sighed. "I couldn't believe how well things were going. We'd made it to the cake, and I thought we would get a great review from all of them. They all gave us such positive feedback."

"I'm sorry things didn't end that way." Suzie eyed the trash can, then looked up at her. "Do you have any theories about what might have happened? Did anyone hang around in the kitchen?"

"Other than you two?" Katrina looked between them. "Not that I saw. But I was going in and out a lot, and I did take a few smoke breaks." She lowered her eyes. "I know it's a bad habit, but I haven't broken it, yet."

"What about when you were outside?" Mary raised her eyebrows. "Did you notice anyone hanging around out there? Someone who wasn't a guest? Someone from town?"

"You think someone from around here might have done it?" Katrina gasped. "Who would do that?"

"We don't think anything in particular," Suzie said. "We're just trying to get a full picture of what might have happened."

"I'm sorry, I didn't see anyone." Katrina looked

over the countertops. "I really have to get it all cleaned. Tasha's been a mess all morning. She's certain that she'll have to close the business." She sighed. "And she might, but until then, I'm hoping to help her keep it running."

"Of course. We'll get out of your way. If you think of anything, though, please let us know," Suzie said.

"I guess it's possible that someone from town could have done it." Katrina began wiping down a counter. "People can hold on to grudges for a long time. Maybe she upset someone in the past."

"Exactly." Suzie narrowed her eyes. "Did you know her?"

"Know her?" Katrina looked up at her. "What do you mean?"

"It's just that we never mentioned that Margret had lived in the area before, but the way you said that made me think that you knew she'd lived around here before. Did you?" Suzie continued to hold her gaze.

"I don't know what you're talking about. I have no idea about where she lived, and I've never met her. I never even met her last night." Katrina continued to wipe the counter.

"I thought I told you two to leave?" Beth called out from the doorway of the kitchen.

Suzie turned to look at her and tried to keep her voice even.

"We're on our way out right now."

"Good." Beth glared at her, then looked at Katrina. "May I speak with you for a few minutes, Katrina?"

"Sure, of course." Katrina put down the cloth and walked over to Beth.

As the two began talking, Mary started toward the door.

Suzie glanced in Beth's direction for a quick second, then ran her fingertips along the top of the small trash can that Katrina had been standing by when they walked in. She loosened the thin, plastic bag that filled it until it slipped free. She thought about just looking in the bag, but she wanted to get out of there as quickly as possible. She held her breath as she wondered if she'd be caught as she lifted the bag out of the trash can and rushed to the door.

Mary held the door open for her, her eyes wide. "Suzie, what are you doing?" She hissed her words.

"Shh!" Suzie hurried through the door with the trash bag clasped in her hands. Once outside, she glanced over her shoulder. "Do you think they noticed?"

"I don't think so." Mary looked toward the door, then back at her. "But why did you take it?"

"Katrina threw something out when we walked in, then she seemed startled to see us. I just want to see what it was. It's probably nothing." Suzie held the trash bag open. Her heart skipped a beat as her gaze settled on a piece of crumpled paper on top of all of the trash.

"Is that Dune House stationery?" Mary whispered.

"Yes, it is." Suzie peered at the paper. "And it looks like it has a list of names on it." She picked it up by the corner and pulled it out of the bag. "I think this is pretty important. It has Margret's name on it."

"Maybe Katrina didn't want it to be found," Mary said.

"Or maybe she just threw it out."

"We can't be sure that's what she threw out, can we?"

"Maybe not. It was near the top, but I jostled the bag when I pulled it out of the trash can. We're going to have to make sure Jason has a chance to look at this. Can you take a picture of it?" Suzie held out the piece of paper.

Mary pulled out her phone and snapped the picture.

"What's that you have there?" Beth stepped out through the back door and settled an authoritative glare on both of them.

CHAPTER 15

Suzie took a step back as she felt the weight of Beth's glare.

"It's just something that we found that might be important to the investigation. It has Margret's name on it, as well as other names and dates." She held the paper out to her. "We were going to give it to you, of course."

"Of course." Beth pulled a glove from her pocket and slipped it on her hand before taking the piece of paper. "Interesting. Tell me where you found it."

Mary held up the bag of trash. "Suzie noticed—"

"I noticed it when I walked past the trash can." Suzie shot a quick glance at Mary, then cleared her throat. "I saw that it was Dune House stationery, and we also found a threatening note written to

Margret on the same stationery. So, I thought it might be important."

"I can see why you thought that." Beth pulled a small plastic bag from her pocket and slipped the paper inside. "What I don't understand is why you would take it outside to look at it, instead of alerting me immediately that you found something. Perhaps if you hadn't touched this and contaminated it, this evidence would be more valuable."

"It was in a trash can." Mary quirked an eyebrow. "I'm pretty sure it was already contaminated."

"That isn't the point, is it?" Beth cut her gaze in Mary's direction, then looked back at Suzie. "I think we have a real problem here."

"I don't have any problem." Suzie slowly folded her arms. "I just want to know what happened to Margret."

"Don't we all?" Beth offered a strained smile. "I heard about you, Suzie, before I was assigned to this precinct."

"You did?" Suzie's confidence faltered. "Why?"

"Why? Because it's quite common knowledge that Jason lets his cousin do whatever she pleases. I knew that as soon as I arrived, I would have to deal with you. And here we are." Beth crossed her arms.

"I get it, Jason favors you, so you think you can get away with anything, but I'm here to do my job. I'm not going to let anything stop me from doing that, or anyone." She held up the plastic bag. "I don't think you were going to give this to me. I can only hope that you were going to give it to Jason. But that doesn't matter. What matters is that I am a police officer investigating this crime. If I make a request of you, I expect you to cooperate. Let's not forget that Margret died in your home. The only reason you haven't been brought in for further questioning is because Jason is certain that neither you nor Mary are involved."

"He did question us." Suzie clenched her jaw. "We aren't involved."

"I don't know that. Jason is the one that is certain you aren't involved." Beth crossed the small distance between them and looked straight into Suzie's eyes. "But I'm not. I think that you have a lot to lose here. Maybe you have a history with Margret. She'd lived in many towns, and so have you. Maybe there is some history between you, and you decided you needed to get rid of her. Whatever the reason was, I think you saw her birthday dinner as an opportunity to get rid of the problem or get revenge, and now, you're eager to pin the crime that you committed on someone else, which is why every time I turn around, you're interfering with my investigation."

"That's nonsense." Mary stepped up beside Suzie. "You may be an officer of the law, but you have no right to talk to us like that. Suzie had nothing to do with this." She squeezed Suzie's shoulder. "Let's go. I'm not going to stand here while she accuses us like this."

"It's not like you're in the clear, Mary." Beth smirked. "You two are in this together, aren't you? I know that you're very good friends."

"So, that means nothing." Suzie tried to keep her voice even.

"Come on, let's go." Mary grabbed Suzie's arm and steered her toward the car.

"Stay out of my investigation, Suzie!" Beth called out as they neared the car. "You too, Mary."

"Who does she think she is?" Suzie opened her car door.

"A very determined police officer." Mary met her eyes across the top of the car. "We need to watch our step. She clearly has a grudge against us, and I think she actually suspects us for this crime. She's not wrong. If the evidence piles up in the right way, there's nothing that Jason can do to protect us.

Suzie, I know she upset you, she upset me, too, but we're going to have to be a little more careful when we're around her."

Suzie looked back in the direction of the shop.

Beth had already disappeared inside.

"You're right, Mary. We'll have to be careful. But if she keeps behaving this way, it's not us that will have to worry about her, it's her that will have to worry about Jason."

Suzie stared at Tasha's business a moment longer, then slid into the driver's seat and pulled the door closed.

CHAPTER 16

"All right, now I know something more is going on here." Mary sat back in the passenger seat and crossed her arms as she looked over at Suzie. "Suzie, I know that look on your face. You're really upset. What is going on between you and Beth?"

"Nothing, I don't even know her." Suzie avoided Mary's gaze as she slid the key into the ignition.

"Don't you start this car." Mary cast a sharp look in her direction. "Suzie, we're not going anywhere until you tell me why you lied to Beth. That's not something you normally do."

"I didn't lie to her." Suzie looked over at her. "What do you mean?"

"You told her that you just found the note in the

trash can. But you told me that you saw Katrina throw something in the trash." Mary held her gaze. "It's not like you to hold back information from the police."

"I know." Suzie bit into her bottom lip, then sat back against her seat. "The thing is, I don't know for sure that Katrina threw that paper away. I just know that she threw something away. If it had been Jason asking me, I would have told him in a second what I suspected, but I just don't trust Beth. I mean the paper might not even be relevant. What if I'm wrong and it wasn't Katrina that threw the paper away, and she gets into trouble because of my mistake?"

"You know you're not wrong. But I can understand your concern. Beth certainly acts like she has something to prove. Still, it's not going to look too good if Jason finds out you didn't tell her the whole truth."

"How would he? You and I were the only people in that kitchen."

"But you do think it was her, right?" Mary took a deep breath. "You know what that means. We have a reason to suspect that Katrina is the one who killed Margret. She helped prepare the food. She could have easily slipped the poison into one dish before it was served."

"I know." Suzie gripped the steering wheel, then pursed her lips.

"It's okay, you can start the car now." Mary buckled her seat belt.

"Thanks." Suzie laughed, then turned the key. "I think we need to find out as much as we can about Katrina. If she did kill Margret, she must have had a reason. We need to find out why Katrina had Margret's name on that piece of paper."

"Well, we can start with what Jason said about Margret living nearby in the past. Maybe Katrina crossed paths with Margret at that time."

"Ten years ago, Katrina would have probably been in her twenties or thirties." Suzie turned out onto the main street. "Let's see what we can turn up about her life around that time."

"Oh, that wasn't too hard." Mary stared down at her phone. "I just did a search on Katrina's name and that range of time. There's quite a sensational news story about herself and a few other people, and a Dolly Carver." She clucked her tongue. "Who looks a lot like Margret might have ten years ago."

"What is the news story about exactly?" Suzie turned into the parking lot of Dune House.

"Katrina accused a company, Future Investments, of swindling her and her husband out of their savings. They claimed the investment would have a threefold return, but the company suddenly shut down and the money disappeared." Mary skimmed the article, then glanced up at Suzie. "Dolly owned the company."

"Are you sure it's Margret?" Suzie parked, then looked over at Mary's phone. "That does look a lot like her. If Katrina really invested all of her money with the company, and it disappeared, and Dolly was to blame, why wasn't Dolly arrested?"

"I think that's a question for Wes." Mary looked up from her phone and spotted him on the front porch of Dune House. "Considering that the crime was investigated by the Parish Police Department."

"Do you think he was involved in the investigation?" Suzie waved to him through the windshield.

"Only one way to find out." Mary stepped out of the car as Wes descended the front steps and crossed the parking lot toward her.

"Things seem to be going smoothly here." Wes glanced over his shoulder at Dune House. "Most of the guests are out and about."

"Good, because I need to speak with you about

this." Mary handed her phone over to him. "Can you come inside for a few minutes?"

"Sure." Wes followed them inside the house. "Ah, I remember this case." He stepped into the living room and skimmed through the information in the article.

"You do? Did you investigate it?" Mary glanced at Suzie, then looked back at him.

"No, it wasn't my area. My partner at the time investigated it. But I do remember the splash it caused. This company swept into town claiming to be the best investment option for the middle-class crowd, and a lot of people invested their money. Some people got smart and pulled their cash back out, but a few invested every penny they had." Wes lowered the phone and looked at Mary. "What does this have to do with Margret's murder, though?"

"Don't you recognize Dolly?" Suzie pointed to the picture on the phone.

"Dolly?" Wes peered at the picture. "Maybe vaguely from when the case was being investigated."

"Oh, that's right, you never actually met Margret!" Mary took the phone from him and made the photograph larger, then showed it to him again. "Suzie and I are certain this is Margret from ten years ago. Jason discovered that she had lived in the area during that time, and she's used different names. We're guessing she used the name Dolly Carver when she lived here, but we haven't confirmed that with him."

"You're saying that the woman killed in Dune House was Dolly Carver?" Wes asked. "And Katrina lost her money in an investment to her?"

"And she didn't mention a thing about knowing Margret from the past." Suzie crossed her arms. "If Mary and I were able to recognize Margret as Dolly, I have no doubt that Katrina recognized her. And wouldn't Margret have recognized Katrina?"

"I would think so," Mary said. "But it was a long time ago. People change."

"This sure gives Katrina a lot of motive." Wes rubbed his hand along his chin as he stared at the photograph.

"What I don't understand is why wasn't Dolly arrested at the time? If she was involved in the crime, why was she allowed to go free?" Mary took her phone back from him and looked down at the picture. "I'm sure it's the same person!"

"As I recall, and my memory may be a bit foggy on this, no one could prove fraud. There was no written assurances. It was just a bad investment. Dolly claimed she lost in the investment, too. If the police weren't able to prove that fraud took place, and the money was ultimately stolen, then they wouldn't have had enough to charge her. I can't remember anything else. I can look into it and find out the details, though. This certainly can't be a coincidence." Wes put his hands in his pockets.

"Yes, please do." Mary scrolled to another picture on her phone and held it up for Wes to see. "We have good reason to believe that Katrina was involved in Margret's death. We found this piece of stationery with Margret's name, as well as a few other names, and dates. We think Katrina probably wrote it."

"Oh, look at that." Suzie pointed to the photo. "It has Lorraine's name on there. The person from Shady Village that organized the trip. I didn't notice before."

"Oh, it does." Mary looked at the phone. "That's interesting."

"Isn't it possible this has something to do with Tasha's catering jobs?" Wes looked over the names. "Maybe they had allergies or something?"

"Maybe." Mary thought about the suggestion. "But Lorraine wasn't here for the dinner."

"We know that a woman was at the motel late last night and dropped the notepad. What if it was

Katrina? Maybe she's the one who wrote the note that you found on the beach, Mary?" Suzie suggested.

"It's possible." Mary narrowed her eyes. "But why would she then take it to the motel? The only connection that we know she has to anyone at the motel is Lorraine because she has her name written down on that piece of paper."

"Lorraine was only here for a few minutes, you're right. I doubt she had any interaction with Katrina then. I doubt Lorraine dealt with Katrina when all of this was set up. I'm sure Lorraine would have spoken to Tasha." Suzie took out her phone. "Let's have a quick look to see if we can find out what those names and dates might mean." After a few minutes, she looked up at Mary and Wes. "Well, it looks like a couple of other people on the list were scammed by Dolly as well."

"So, does that mean that Lorraine was also involved?" Mary's eyes widened. "Because her name was on the list."

"I can't find any indication of that." Suzie continued to tap on her phone. "But if she was, it would certainly give her a motive. Maybe Jason has found a link and more information about the people on the list."

"Maybe. I'll look into them more as well," Wes said.

"Thank you." Mary glanced around at the end tables in the living room, dotted with empty water bottles. "I'd better do some cleaning up. It might help me to get my thoughts flowing. I sure hope that Jason figures out where the poison came from, soon, or at least clears the kitchen, so that we can go back to eating and serving food from the kitchen."

"I'll check with him." Suzie pulled her phone from her pocket. "I'll take Pilot out for a walk, too, and when I get back, I'll help tidy up."

"Maybe by then we'll have figured this out." Mary picked up a water bottle.

"I've got to head back to Parish, but if you need me for anything, I'm just a phone call away." Wes kissed her goodbye.

"Thank you." Mary smiled as she watched him leave. Despite all of the chaos roaming through her mind, his presence made everything feel so much calmer. She'd resisted the idea of getting into a new relationship after her marriage failed, but Wes had found his way in when she least expected it. She'd always be glad he did.

CHAPTER 17

s Mary heard Suzie and Pilot head out through the front door, she turned her attention back to the mess in the living room. As she dusted the furniture, she noticed a few of the pieces of furniture had been moved out of place. She pushed one of the easy chairs back into position beside a wooden end table. The chair moved a bit more than she intended and bumped into the table. The drawer in the table popped open a few inches. She froze at the sight of a notepad inside. Had someone put it there? If so, who? She slid the drawer open the rest of the way and carefully lifted the notepad out. It was Dune House stationery. The top page had no writing on it, but it did look as if at least one page had been torn off.

As Mary looked at the paper, she realized it was just another dead end. There was no way to know who had this out here. It wasn't from one of the rooms. Suzie had checked them. Maybe it had been there from before. Mary ran her hand along the surface of the paper to smooth it down. As she did, she felt ridges against the soft skin of her palm. She peered closer at the paper and noticed indentations.

"What do you have there, Mary?" Suzie stepped into the living room with Pilot at her side. "You found another pad of paper?"

"Yes, it was in this drawer." Mary continued to study the paper. "I think someone wrote so hard on it that they left traces of their words behind."

"Oh, I know a trick that might help us with that." Suzie pulled open the drawer and rummaged around inside until she found a pencil. "Set it down here on the table."

"Okay." Mary set the notepad down, then watched as Suzie began to run the pencil lightly back and forth across the paper. As she did, the indentations in the paper remained untouched by the pencil. As each letter appeared, Mary began to read the words that Suzie uncovered.

Because of your behavior, Margret, I have nothing left. You can never be forgiven. You'll pay for what you did.

"Suzie!" Mary patted her shoulder. "Those are the same words from the note Wes and I found on the beach."

"Are you sure?" Suzie set the pencil down and skimmed over the words she'd revealed. "You're right!"

"Only now, we can read the whole thing."

"Whoever wrote it must have been pretty upset at the time, that's why the letters carried through to the next sheet of paper."

Mary skimmed to the bottom of the note.

"Is that a signature?"

"I think it is." Suzie held the notepad up and squinted at the squiggle of letters. "I think the first letter is a 'V.'"

"And there's definitely an 'r.'" Mary's eyes widened at the same time Suzie gasped.

"Vera!" they declared the name in unison.

"Vera wrote the note?" Suzie set the notepad back down. "She must have been very angry with Margret to write things like that, but she doesn't say what she's angry about in the note."

"Lucky for us, we can just ask her." Mary snatched up the notepad. "She hasn't said a word about having a grudge against Margret, at least not to us, which means she's hiding something. I think we should talk to her about it."

"I agree, but Mary, before we do, we need to consider the fact that she might be the one who killed Margret. If she wrote this note, she definitely had a reason to hate Margret, which means she's just as much a suspect as Greta, and Katrina. You heard Wes, we need to be careful. We still don't know what poison was used to kill Margret, and if Vera is the killer, she might still have some left."

"That's true." Mary looked up at her. "Jason didn't have any update?"

"He said he's hoping to have some more results soon." Suzie glanced around the living room, then out into the entranceway. "Vera might be in her room. Maybe we can talk to her. I need to replenish some things in the rooms, anyway."

"Good plan." Mary picked up the pad of paper. "For now we need to keep this somewhere safe, so that we can hand it over to Jason. He'll be happy to know we found the full note. Let's try to speak to her."

"Do you think that Margret might have swindled Vera, too? That would explain why she's so angry with her." Suzie gestured to the large desk in the entranceway. "Put it in the file drawer. We can lock it. No one will be able to get to it."

"Good idea." Mary walked over to the desk and slid the notepad inside the drawer. She checked to make sure it was locked. "From what I understand, Vera didn't even know Margret very long, Margret had just recently moved into Shady Village. If she had recognized her from the past, why wouldn't she have turned her in to the police?"

"Maybe for the same reason that Katrina didn't. She was more interested in revenge than a jail sentence. But wouldn't Margret have recognized Katrina and Vera if she knew them from the past?"

"I would imagine so." Mary followed Suzie up the stairs in the direction of Vera's room.

Suzie knocked on the door. When there was no reply, she knocked again.

When there was still no answer, she slid her key into the lock. She turned the key, then the knob. The door swung open.

"What are you doing in here?" a sleepy voice called out from the bed.

CHAPTER 18

*S*tartled, Suzie took a step back.

"Vera, I'm so sorry to disturb you. We knocked, but you obviously didn't hear us. Mary and I are just doing some tidying up and wanted to see if you had any towels or anything else that needed to be replaced or replenished. I had no idea you were in here. Again, I'm so sorry."

Vera sat up in the bed and gazed at the two of them as they hovered in the doorway.

"I do have some towels that need washing. Just give me a second. I'm still surfacing from my power nap." She swung her feet over the side of the bed and yawned. "I've been taking them since I was twenty years old. They help me stay active and sharp." She slid her feet into slippers beside the bed, then stood up. "I have a pile of towels. I'm afraid I used more than I realized. I've been in the water a few times."

"You have?" Suzie shivered at the thought. "Isn't it too cold for you? These fall temperatures keep me out of the ocean."

"Oh, I don't mind." Vera smiled. "Once you get into the water, you get used to it. Besides, I couldn't pass it up. It looked so beautiful, and I love to swim." She walked over to a pile of towels in the corner of the room. "Let me get those for you."

"That's okay." Mary walked over and began gathering up the damp towels. She noticed that one was soaked through.

"I'm sorry it's so wet. I filled up a water bottle to water a little plant I brought with me." Vera pointed toward the bottle. "But I knocked over the water, so I used the towel to wipe it up. I'm so clumsy now that I'm getting older."

"Oh, don't worry about that." Suzie waved her hand through the air.

"I know it's weird to bring with a plant." Vera gave a short laugh. "But I love a bit of greenery in my room. It helps me relax."

"Oh, I agree. I find the environment I'm in to be

so important to my mood." Suzie looked around the room in search of the plant.

"It's in the bathroom, now." Vera pointed at the bathroom. "The water was making a mess."

"Okay." Suzie met Vera's eyes. She decided if she wanted to find out the truth about the note, she needed to start asking her some questions. "Vera, how well did you know Margret?"

"I've been asked that so many times." Vera laughed. "I keep saying the same thing, I didn't. I didn't really know her. I knew of her, because there was so much gossip about how she'd come to live at Shady Village. About how she conned her way in there. But as far as knowing her personally, I never had the chance to."

"Are you sure about that?" Mary bundled up the laundry in her arms and looked across the top of the pile at Vera. "You weren't perhaps angry at her for any reason?"

"Why are you asking that?" Vera's voice lowered. "Why would I be angry at her?"

"Well, like you said, she conned her way into getting a home at Shady Village. Maybe you didn't like that?" Suzie studied her expression and noticed the tension in her face. "Vera, if there was something between you and Margret that you haven't told the police, you need to admit to it. Things will only get more complicated the longer you hide it."

"I'm not hiding anything." Vera gasped, then glared at them both.

"We came across something, a note written by you, that sounded very angry. We just want to give you a chance to explain yourself before we alert the police about the note," Suzie said.

"Oh no!" Vera sank down onto the edge of her bed. "How did you find it?"

"So, you did write it?" Mary glanced over at Suzie, then looked back at Vera. "What were you so angry at Margret about?"

"Yes, I wrote it." Vera sighed. "I do that sometimes when I have pent-up emotions that I don't want. I write letters to the people I'm upset with to get my frustrations out. But I never send them. I wrote that letter to Margret, then I took it out to the beach with me, and I planned to burn it. It's what I usually do, you know, to release the negative emotions and let go of the grudge. But before I could burn it, the wind snatched it away from me." She pressed her hand against her stomach and shuddered. "I had assumed it would end up in the ocean. No one was ever meant to read it."

"We did." Suzie stepped closer to her. "Why did you write it?"

"I told you, I just wanted to get my feelings out. It's like journaling, but there's something more cathartic about writing it in the form of a letter and burning it. I was talking to Greta about it, and I was upset, so she gave me her notepad. She said I should go do what I normally do to feel better." Vera looked down at her hands. "I know it doesn't look too good, the things I wrote, but I never would have said them to Margret face-to-face. I'm really not that kind of person."

"Why did you write it in the first place?" Mary shifted the laundry in her arms. "Why were you so angry at her?"

"I'd rather not speak ill of the dead." Vera clasped her hands together on her lap and stared down at them.

"I think you already have." Mary set the towels back down on the floor and sat down on the bed beside Vera. "I know that you didn't mean to. You never meant for those words to be read by anyone else, but they have been, Vera. The police are going to need an explanation, or they may begin to suspect that you had something to do with Margret's murder."

"Me?" Vera looked up at her and gasped. "I would never do something like that!"

"Maybe, but you're going to have to give them some kind of explanation for the hatred that was scribbled on that paper." Suzie walked closer to her.

"Okay, okay." Vera pressed her hands on the sides of her face. "I'm a trusting person. My late husband always warned me that I was too trusting. He said that I always thought the best of people, even when they wanted to hurt me. He was right." She took a deep breath. "Since he's been gone, I've been so lonely, so I've been having people over to my place as much as possible, just to fill the empty space."

"I understand that." Mary patted her hand.

"I invited Greta and a few others to dinner one night, and Margret invited herself." Vera bit into her bottom lip. "Greta tried to get me to refuse to let her in, but I'm just not like that. I can't hurt someone or reject them right to their face like that. It would be so cruel. So, I let her in. We suffered through dinner, then everyone left. When I started preparing for bed, I took off my bracelet to put it into my jewelry box and found that my jewelry box was missing. It wasn't on my dresser." She shivered as tears filled her eyes.

"You think someone stole it?" Suzie asked.

"My wedding band was in that jewelry box. I'd just decided to stop wearing it the week before. I was trying to take steps to open my life to new relationships. I didn't care about any of the other jewelry. It was expensive, yes, but it didn't mean anything. It was my wedding band going missing that broke my heart. I knew my jewelry box had been there before dinner because I'd put my bracelet on after I'd gotten dressed, just a few minutes before guests began arriving. I immediately suspected Margret. I knew everyone else that I'd invited to the dinner pretty well, and I knew that none of them would steal from me."

"Did you call the police?" Mary patted her hand. "That must have been terrible to have someone steal from you like that."

"It was, but I didn't want to involve the police. I knew that Margret would deny it, and I was worried that she would get rid of the jewelry, including my wedding band. So, I went to Greta. She agreed with me that it was probably Margret that stole the jewelry. I begged her to talk to her, to see if she could convince Margret to give me back the ring. She said she would try, but she doubted it would work." Vera took a deep breath, then sighed.

"I never got it back. Now Margret is dead, and I'm sure I'll never see it again."

"I'm so sorry." Suzie sat down on the other side of her. "Losing something that special to you must have hurt a lot. But it also must have made you very angry."

"I didn't kill her." Vera gripped the edge of the bed and looked up at Suzie. "Do you hear me? I don't care what you might be thinking. I did not kill her! I had accepted it. I told myself I had to move on, and that I needed to focus on the future, not the past. Did it hurt? Yes, of course. But there was nothing I could do about it."

"I still don't understand why you didn't call the police." Mary frowned. "If you knew that it was Margret, I'm sure they could have searched her house or something."

"Greta warned me not to involve them. She said that Margret has a way of getting away with everything. She also said that she could be very vicious, and she didn't want to see Margret turn against me." Vera stood up from the bed. "All I wanted was that ring. I didn't want to cause a huge feud. I wanted excitement in my life, not fear."

"Didn't you suspect that Greta might be in on it? Maybe she steered you away from calling the police in an attempt to protect her sister." Mary looked up at her. "When was your jewelry stolen?"

"About a week before the trip. That's why I was still so angry about it, and then to be expected to celebrate her birthday, that just pushed me over the edge." Vera turned to face them both. "I've known Greta for over a year. She's never been anything but kind to me. She can be brash, and she has a strange sense of humor, but she's been nothing but helpful to me as I grieved the loss of my husband. She lost her husband as well, many years ago, but we bonded over the same feelings. There's no way that she would have been in on the theft, and I knew that if there was any way she could get the ring back for me, she would." She used the back of her hand to wipe her eyes. "I know none of this will make sense to the police. How can I ever explain it? I know you have to tell them. But I didn't do this. I didn't hurt Margret. Do you think they'll arrest me?"

"I don't think you have to worry. Jason is going to do what the evidence tells him to do. He's only going to be interested in arresting the killer." Suzie stood up and walked toward the door. "We just want to find out who killed Margret."

"She's right." Mary picked up the laundry again.

"If you think of anything that might help us figure that out, let us know right away."

"I will." Vera sprawled back out on the bed. "Just let them know when they show up with their handcuffs, I'll be right here."

"I'm sure it will be okay." Suzie tried to reassure her but didn't know how it would all turn out.

CHAPTER 19

Suzie held the door of Vera's room open for Mary as they stepped out, then closed it behind her.

"What are we going to do?" Mary looked into Suzie's eyes. "You know as well as I do that she makes the perfect suspect."

"I know." Suzie grabbed a few of the towels from Mary's arms. "But I don't think she did it. Why would she be so honest with us about the jewelry being stolen if she's guilty? She had to know that made for a good motive."

"True, but she also needed an explanation for that note she wrote."

"At least, the fact that Greta gave her the notepad explains why we didn't find it missing. I never looked for the notepad in her room because it was ransacked." Suzie headed down the steps to the first floor.

"I think we need to speak to Greta. If she knew about the theft, then why didn't she say anything else about it?"

"Vera did say that they had bonded over the past year. Maybe Greta was afraid that if she told the police about the theft, it would make Vera look guilty of Margret's murder." Suzie reached the bottom of the steps and turned down the hall to the first door. "All I know for sure is that we have a few good suspects, and no actual evidence to point to one of them." She stepped through the door into the laundry room and dropped the towels into the open washer. "At least now we know who wrote that note, but we still can't be sure who wrote down Margret's name along with those dates. Although we believe it probably was Katrina."

"Probably." Suzie set the box of detergent down on top of the dryer. "You're right, we need to find out from Greta why she didn't tell the police about the theft. I'm not convinced that she was trying to protect Vera. I think there might have been something more underhanded at play." She measured out the detergent, then added it to the washer. "Let's see what she has to say."

"Maybe it will shake her up a little that we know about it, and she might let something slip." Mary set the washer, then started it. "I heard some voices outside when we were coming down the stairs, I think one of them belonged to Greta." She led the way to the side porch.

As Mary slid the door open, she spotted a group of people at a picnic table on the wraparound porch. Greta sat at one end of the table with Chip, John, and Beryl across from her.

"Listen, the sooner we figure out what happened to Margret, the sooner we can all get out of here. I don't mean to accuse anyone of anything, I'm just asking where you were while dinner was being prepared." Greta shrugged.

"That sounds like an accusation to me!" Chip stood up. "I won't stand for it, either. Everyone here knows that you were the one who had a grudge against your sister. We should be the ones asking you where you were!"

"I was on the beach, then I was playing outside with Pilot on the way back. I was outside the whole time. There, now you know." Greta clasped her hands together. "I also know that I didn't see any of you out there on the beach at the same time I was out there. So where were you?"

"Chip and I were at the frozen yogurt place." Beryl stood up.

"Sweets before dinner?" John clucked his tongue.

"I couldn't eat on the bus. I can never eat on a moving vehicle. I get travel sickness, you know. Anyway, I was starving, and I had no idea what to expect from dinner. I found out that they hired a caterer, but I couldn't find any reviews of her work. I guess the business has just opened. So, I wanted to make sure I had something in my stomach just in case I didn't like what was served for dinner." Beryl wrapped her hand around Chip's. "Relax, honey, she's just trying to play detective. There's nothing to get offended about."

"Did I say I was offended?" Chip looked over at her.

"You kind of implied it with that behavior," John said.

"We should go and relax for a while, Chip." Beryl clung to his arm. "I want to do some reading."

"I need a break. I'll be on the beach until dinner." John waved his hand as he walked away.

Once Suzie and Mary were alone with Greta, Suzie walked over to her.

"Are you conducting your own investigation into who killed your sister?"

"So what if I am?" Greta scowled.

"Well, perhaps you should look at the most likely suspect who you seem to be protecting." Suzie leaned against the picnic table.

"I have no idea what you're talking about." Greta stood up and started toward the door.

"Just a second, please." Suzie stepped up beside her. "I just have a couple of things I want to know."

"Oh, really?" Greta stopped and turned toward Suzie with a sharp glare. "And what makes you think that you're entitled to know anything?"

"Greta, we're just trying to help. It seems to me that you do have an interest in finding out who hurt your sister. You were just asking the others about it. So now we need you to work with us, so we can try to help figure this all out." Mary stepped up on the other side of her.

"I think that you both just need to stay out of it. It has nothing to do with you." Greta took another step toward the house.

"It has everything to do with us. Your sister was killed under our roof, at our dinner table." Suzie walked next to her. "I tried to save her." She held up her hands. "I gave her chest compressions."

"Oh, don't flatter yourself." Greta waved her hand through the air. "We wouldn't have even been here, if it wasn't for that woman pushing so hard for Lorraine to bring the group here."

"What woman?" Mary narrowed her eyes.

"There was a woman that came to Shady Village and left a bunch of pamphlets about Dune House. She talked Lorraine's ear off about what a good place it would be to take the trip to this year. You must know her, right? She must work for your marketing team?"

"We are the marketing team." Suzie's mind swam with the information. "We didn't send anyone out to drum up business."

"Well, someone was there, and she convinced Lorraine to come here for the trip. We had originally planned on somewhere with a casino, which, no offense, would have been a lot more fun." Greta crossed her arms.

"No offense taken." Mary gave a short laugh. "Do you know this woman's name?"

"No, but Lorraine might." Greta started to walk off. "Are you both done harassing me?"

"Wait, just a few more questions." Mary stepped

in front of her. "We spoke with Vera. We know that she wrote a terrible letter to Margret. We also know that she held a grudge against her for stealing her wedding band. She told us that you knew about the note and the theft. Why didn't you tell the police about that?"

"Why should I? I don't work for them." Greta glared at Mary. "They have never done a single thing to help me in my entire life. In fact, they've always just made everything worse."

"But didn't it cross your mind that Vera might have been the one to kill Margret, since she wanted her wedding ring back?" Suzie asked.

"And how would she get the ring back, if Margret was dead? It's not like she left anything to me. I knew that Vera didn't kill Margret. She doesn't have that kind of makeup. She acts tough, but she'd never hurt anyone. I didn't want the police interrogating her over something that had nothing to do with my sister's death. As far as I'm concerned, you shouldn't tell the police, either. It will just distract them from finding the real killer." Greta pushed past Suzie. "Now, I'm going inside." She reached for the door handle.

"Just one second, please." Mary pulled her phone out of her pocket. "Can you please just look at one photograph for me? We're trying to figure out exactly how Margret knew this person. Maybe you'll recognize her." She displayed a photograph of Katrina.

"Well, that's her." Greta peered at the photograph on the screen.

"What do you mean that's her? Do you remember her from about ten years ago?" Suzie's heart skipped a beat. "Or from yesterday when she was at Dune House?"

"No, I remember her from about two weeks ago, when she showed up at Shady Village with all the pamphlets. She's your best promoter." Greta looked up from the phone and straight into Suzie's eyes. "I also saw her here last night. Is she a friend of yours?"

"Not exactly." Mary's hand trembled as she slid her phone back into her pocket. "We're going to need you to confirm this with Jason."

"If you want to confirm it, talk to Lorraine. If it involves the police, I will not be involved." Greta jerked the door to the house open and strode inside.

CHAPTER 20

"*C*an you believe that?" Mary looked over at Suzie with wide eyes. "Katrina convinced Lorraine to come here? Do you know what that means?"

"It means she wanted Margret here." Suzie reached for her phone. "I think we should call Jason and tell him about what Greta just told us and about the note."

"Okay." Mary nodded as Suzie dialed his number as she walked back toward the picnic table.

"Suzie?" Jason answered.

"I'm putting you on speakerphone, Jason." Suzie switched to speakerphone and set the phone down on the picnic table. "We have something to tell you." She met Mary's eyes before continuing.

"We've discovered who wrote the note that Mary and Wes found on the beach, and it wasn't Katrina."

"That verifies her story. She insisted that she didn't know anything about the note that was found on the beach, or the note that you turned over to Beth." Jason paused, then cleared his throat. "Beth was quite upset that you took it out of the trash can without telling her, and that you didn't volunteer the note immediately to her."

"Listen, Jason, I know that she has a badge, but I don't trust her." Suzie sighed. "I'm happy to share anything I come across with you, but I think it's best if Beth and I stay out of each other's way."

"I agree. So, who wrote the note?" Jason's voice sounded strained as it carried through the speaker on the phone.

"One of the guests, Vera. We also were able to find out what the rest of the note said." Suzie explained the trick she'd used to reveal the entire note, and the alleged theft of her jewelry. "I'll make sure it gets to you."

"That was very clever, Suzie. I'm going to send someone over to speak with Vera again." Jason's keyboard clacked in the background.

"You may also want to go back to Katrina again.

We just had Greta tell us that she went to Shady Village and convinced Lorraine to travel here."

"Wow, that is very interesting." Jason's voice raised slightly.

"I would talk to Lorraine about it first, though, as Greta is refusing to cooperate with the police." Suzie paused. "Apparently, she's had some bad experiences."

"I can understand that. From what I've been able to piece together of Margret's police record, she's never been convicted of a crime despite many arrests. I imagine Greta lost faith in the system after all of that," Jason said.

"Or maybe Greta has helped her get away with her crimes all these years." Mary clicked her fingers together. "She knew about the jewelry theft and didn't tell anyone about it. She's clearly used to hiding things."

"That's true." Jason sighed. "All right, I'm going to speak to Lorraine to start with."

"Do you know what type of poison was used, yet?" Suzie asked.

"Yes, convallatoxin. It's from lily of the valley. A common but highly poisonous plant. It causes a very quick reaction. It means, as we suspected, she was poisoned at some time during the dinner."

"A plant?" Suzie's heart pounded as she recalled the plant Vera had mentioned. "You still don't know what the poison was in?"

"No. But we do know that it was ingested. It had to be in her food or drink. Because of her age, and the fact she had existing health conditions, it caused rapid death. It's possible it wouldn't have caused death in someone else. Like I said, it's not the best lead. We know how she died now, but it doesn't get us any closer to the killer. The plant is easy to access, so it's going to be hard to narrow down the killer that way."

"At least it's something." Suzie looked across the table at Mary.

"Hopefully, I'll find out something new from Katrina or Lorraine." Jason ended the call.

"All I can think about is Vera having a plant in her room." Suzie slid her phone into her pocket. "We should try and see the plant. Maybe we can work out if it's that lily of the valley."

"We can. But I think she's still up there, so that might prove difficult. I think we should start by talking to Katrina. I can't get it out of my mind that it looks like Katrina worked very hard to get

Margret here. Not only does she have a strong motive, but she's been lying to us this whole time," Mary said.

"Okay. But since Jason has already questioned her, I'm not so sure that she'll give us any other information. She denied any knowledge of the list of names and dates we found in the trash can. But maybe she's not the only one that we can talk to about it."

"You want to speak to her husband?" Mary asked. "That makes sense. I'm sure he'll want to protect her, but maybe his lies won't line up with Katrina's."

"Let's go find out. He might not be home, or Katrina might be with him, but I think we should try to speak to him." Suzie started toward the stairs.

"It's getting late, now, Suzie," Mary said. "We need to organize the dinner. Lorraine said she would order food from Cheney's. We just have to pick it up and set it out on the porch." Cheney's was a small Italian restaurant in town.

"You're right." Suzie looked at her watch. "I didn't realize how late it was. We'll go first thing tomorrow."

CHAPTER 21

The following morning, after arranging breakfast from the bakery again, Suzie and Mary headed straight for Katrina's house.

"I wish we had learned something more last night or this morning from the guests." Suzie turned onto the main road.

"Me, too. Everyone seemed so quiet."

"They pretty much ate and went straight to bed. Then only a couple came down for breakfast this morning." Suzie stopped at a traffic light.

"I think they're tired from all of this and are ready to move on." Mary peered through the windshield.

"I think you're right. So let's go through what we think might have happened between Katrina and Margret. Katrina had all of her money swindled from her. Clearly, she blamed Margret, even though the police let her off without any charges. So, she decided to take matters into her own hands. She found out that Margret was living at Shady Village and went there to convince Lorraine to take a trip here." Suzie turned down the road that led to Katrina's house. "But why? Why did she want to bring her back here? Why not just kill her there?"

"That's a good question," Mary said. "There had to be a reason that she went to all of the trouble of such an elaborate ruse."

"Exactly." Suzie parked in the driveway behind a car. "It looks like Katrina isn't home. I bet Jason has her down at the station for questioning again. This might be our best chance to find out what her husband knows."

"Let's hope he's willing to talk." Mary stepped out of the car and walked toward the door. "If he's loyal to her, he may not say a word to us."

"That's true." Suzie followed her up to the door. "And he might even be involved. He lost just as much to the con. We should both be on guard." She knocked on the door.

The door swung open as if he might have been

watching through the window. "Yes?" He peered out at the two of them.

"Is Katrina here?" Mary asked.

"No." He frowned. "The police have taken her in for questioning again."

"Well, we were hoping to speak with you about Katrina. I'm Suzie, and this is my friend, Mary." Suzie gestured to Mary who stood beside her. They had been to a few of the same community events, and she had seen him around town. She had spoken to him in passing a couple of times, but as they had never been introduced properly, she wasn't sure if he would recognize or remember them.

"I know who you are." Phil sighed as he stepped back from the door. "I've heard so much about both of you. Come inside."

Suzie hesitated. It wasn't the greeting she had expected. Instead of resisting their presence, he seemed eager to have them inside his house. Did he plan to cause them harm?

"Thank you, Mr. Smith." Suzie took a cautious step inside.

"Call me Phil." He led them over to a dining room table cluttered with papers. "My name is Phil."

"It's nice to meet you properly, Phil." Mary sat

down in one of the wooden chairs, then winced. "I suppose not like this, though."

"No, not like this." Phil sat down across from them. "Look, I know why you're here. You're upset because Margret was killed in your house, and you think that Katrina did it."

"We think she might have done it," Suzie said. "But we're not here for revenge, or because we're holding a grudge. We're here because we want to find out the truth about what happened to Margret. Do you have any idea why your wife would have done this?"

"First, my wife didn't do this." Phil looked at each of them in turn. "I know it looks that way. But she didn't. She never would have killed Margret."

"How can you be so sure? Didn't you lose all of your savings to her? Didn't it cause great difficulties in your life? Don't you think your wife might have wanted revenge for that?" Suzie tried to meet his eyes, but he stared down at the papers in front of him.

"From what we understand, Margret got away with everything. That had to be infuriating." Mary scooted her chair closer to the table and began looking over the papers scattered across it.

"It was. Of course it was." Phil ran his hands

across his face and sighed. "Katrina became obsessed with it. I pleaded with her to just let it go. But she couldn't."

"Because she was so angry." Suzie clasped her hands together. "She wanted Margret to pay for what she did."

"You have no idea." Phil rested his elbows on the table and leaned forward. "It wasn't just about the money, though that was a huge part of it. It was that she pretended to be our friend. A motherly figure that was helping us out. We trusted her. We invited her into our home. We invited her to family events. She got my brother involved as well, and he invested everything he had. He and his wife haven't spoken to either of us ever since. What this woman did, ruined our entire lives, not just our financial lives."

"I'm so sorry to hear that." Mary sat back in her chair. "No one should ever have to endure losing contact with family members."

"You're right. That's when all this started." Phil gestured to the papers on the table. "One day Katrina announced that she couldn't continue to live with this woman roaming free. She began researching her and finding out everything she could about her. It didn't take long before she figured out that she had been using a fake name, and then later she found out that she used several fake names. She began connecting her to many different crimes. She'd conned so many people, ruined so many lives over the years."

"We found this list of names with dates on it." Suzie showed him the photo of the note on her phone. "Does this have to do with that?"

"Yes, Katrina had started keeping records of the people who had been hurt. She had hoped that she would be able to gather enough evidence against her that the police would have to do something about it. I'm sure the dates on that paper correlate to some of her research. I've been sitting here since the police left, trying to sort it all out. She has kept records of names, dates, locations. But they're not very organized." Phil shoved the papers across the table and groaned. "It doesn't matter anyway. It only makes her look more guilty."

"Wow, she has done a lot of research." Mary glanced at the papers.

"Look, I'm only sharing this with you because I thought you might help me. That you might help Katrina. She had such nice things to say about you. She was so excited to work with you. She told me, when the police took her away, that you two would help, if I asked you to." Phil swung his hand over the stacks of paper. "I thought maybe you could help me make sense of this. Maybe there's a clue of who killed Margret in there."

"Of course. We can try." Mary glanced over the papers. "Sorry I have to ask this. Are you sure she didn't just snap? Maybe she couldn't take the idea of Margret getting away with it again. Maybe she decided to take matters into her own hands."

"Never!" Phil shook his head.

"Okay." Suzie pointed at the papers. "Can we take these with us? We really need to get back to Dune House and make sure everything is okay with our guests."

"Okay. I prefer they don't leave here, but I understand." Phil looked between them.

"Thank you." Suzie picked up some of the papers. "We'll let you know if we find anything."

Mary picked up the rest and headed out the door.

"Thank you." Phil closed the door behind them.

Once they'd settled in the car, Mary looked over at Suzie. "Wow, Katrina certainly seems to have an unhealthy obsession."

"She does." Suzie started the car and backed out of the driveway.

"Phil seemed to want to offer the documents up." Mary tapped her fingers against her knee. "Perhaps we're looking at this the wrong way."

"What do you mean?" Suzie continued down the street.

"I mean, we've been suspecting Katrina this whole time, but her husband could have done this. Maybe Phil is giving us this information to implicate his wife. It's possible, right?"

"Sure, it's possible. But we still can't prove it. And how would he have gotten the poison in the food or drinks?" Suzie asked.

"Good question."

CHAPTER 22

"*L*ook at this, Suzie." Mary glanced at the papers. "This is like the list we think Katrina threw out. It also has some dates and other names on it, and it has a very familiar name on it."

"It does?"

"Freddy Bledsoe."

"Isn't that the bus driver?" Suzie gasped.

"Yes." Mary glanced over the paper again. "If this is a part of Katrina's research into who Margret scammed, then why would she have him on a list?"

"That's what we need to find out. I did search if he had any connection to Margret, and I couldn't find one." Suzie turned onto the main road. "Freddy wasn't much help last time, but if he knows that his name is in the middle of this investigation, maybe he will be this time."

"Maybe." Mary looked at the papers. "From these stacks of papers, I'd guess that Katrina had been investigating Margret for years. It really was an obsession."

"Would you have done anything different?" Suzie glanced over at her. "If someone had stolen every last dime from you, and from your family, would you have just accepted it and moved on?"

"Probably not." Mary smiled some. "I don't think either of us would have."

"Maybe you wouldn't have been obsessed, but you would be angry, resentful. That's why I don't think it's the investigating that makes me suspect her. It's the fact that she conned Lorraine into choosing Dune House for the trip. It appears as if she went to a lot of trouble to make sure that Margret made it here. Why?" Suzie turned into the parking lot of the motel.

"Maybe because it had meaning to her. She wanted to bring Margret back to the place where she'd stolen from her, so she could steal her life?" Mary scrunched up her nose. "It seems a bit ridiculous, but who knows what she was thinking at that point."

"Hopefully, Jason is getting some truth from her." Suzie parked in front of Freddy's motel room. "Do you think he'll let us in?"

"Only one way to find out." Mary stepped out of the car. "Look, there's Lorraine, coming out of Freddy's room."

Lorraine froze at the sight of the two women.

"Hello, there." She looked over at them.

"Lorraine, we're just here to speak with Freddy." Suzie tipped her head toward the motel room. "Is he in there?"

"Yes. I just finished letting him know that we're going to have to stay another night." Lorraine winced as she met Suzie's eyes. "Is that okay?"

"Yes, of course." Suzie waved her hand. "The guests can stay as long as the police need them to."

"Thanks." Lorraine sighed with relief.

"Are you doing okay?" Suzie stepped up onto the walkway. "This must be a lot for you to handle."

"It is. I spoke to Detective Allen just before about Katrina convincing me to bring the group here, and to use Tasha for the catering." Lorraine rubbed her hand along her arm and shivered. "It's hard to believe that Margret's killer might have manipulated me like that. But at least now we have some idea of who did this. It makes sense. She was an assistant to the caterer, right? She could have easily poisoned Margret's food."

"Yes. Although, I don't think the police are sure it was her, just yet," Mary said.

"Maybe not, but from what I understand, the police intend to arrest her." Lorraine continued to her room.

"Do you really think Jason is arresting Katrina?" Mary followed Suzie to Freddy's door.

"It makes sense if he is. He has plenty of evidence against her." Suzie knocked on the door.

"What did you forget, Lorraine?" Freddy swung the door open. "Oh, it's you two. Why?"

"Freddy, we just want to talk to you about Katrina." Suzie looked into his eyes and studied his reaction to the name.

"The crazy caterer that killed Margret?" Freddy raised his eyebrows. "Why do you want to talk to me about her?"

"Had you ever met her before?" Suzie held his gaze.

"No." Freddy leaned against the doorway and stared back at her. "I didn't stay for dinner, remember?"

"I do. But for some reason Katrina had your name written down on a piece of paper. We're trying to figure out why that was." Suzie glanced at Mary, then looked back at him. "Do you think you might have met her before and just don't remember?" She showed him a photo of her on her phone from the catering website.

"I doubt it. She's a looker. I notice those kinds of things." Freddy crossed his arms. "What does it matter if she had my name written down? She's the one who killed Margret."

"Maybe it seems that way. But sometimes things are not as they seem," Suzie said.

"And sometimes boredom can lead to overthinking. I think you two should get back to changing sheets and fluffing pillows and leave the policing to the experts." Freddy started to close the door.

"Wait." Suzie pushed on the door. "Freddy, this is serious. Katrina had been doing research on everyone who was harmed by Margret's cons. Are you sure she wouldn't have had a reason to connect you to that?"

Freddy swung the door open a little farther and sighed. "I had nothing to do with any of this. I'm just the bus driver. Now, if you don't mind, I have some laundry to get to." He gestured to a pile of clothes with a small box of laundry detergent on top. But it was a pair of gardening gloves beside the clothes that caught Suzie's attention. "I wasn't planning on staying this long, so I'm going to need some fresh clothes."

"Right." Mary took a step back. "Of course. We don't want to hold you up."

Suzie stepped away from the door as well. "The offer still stands, Freddy. If you need anything, just let us know."

"Thanks. But I'm the type of person that takes care of myself." Freddy pushed the door closed.

CHAPTER 23

Suzie turned back toward the car.

"Did you see the gardening gloves?"

"Yes, but that doesn't mean anything. Maybe he uses them when he puts gas in the bus or when he works on the bus. I know that Margret was poisoned by a plant, but they're just gloves. They might be used for gardening or other things."

"True. I still think Katrina is the best suspect." Suzie reached for her car door. "Or maybe both Katrina and Phil. He certainly seemed to want to defend her, but why?"

"It might just be a sign of how much he loves his wife and believes she's innocent." Mary pulled open the passenger side door. "Unfortunately, we know for a fact that Katrina has been lying this entire time. That makes it pretty clear that she's guilty."

"I agree. But Jason still has to prove it." Suzie settled in the driver's seat. "We still don't know exactly how Margret was poisoned."

"That's true, but from the timing, we do know that Margret had to ingest the poison at Dune House. We know for certain that Katrina had access to the food, but as far as we know, Freddy was not there." Mary gazed out through the windshield as Suzie pulled out onto the street. "As much as Phil wants to protest, everything points to Katrina."

"Yes, it does." Suzie turned in the direction of the police station. "And I think it's time we make sure that Jason knows everything about Katrina that we do. If we miss sharing even the smallest detail with him, it might mean that Katrina will get away with murder."

"I can understand why Katrina would want to kill Margret. What I don't understand, though, is the way she did it." Mary frowned. "She just got hired by Tasha, who had just opened her business. Why would she risk all of that to poison Margret? She had plenty of opportunities to hurt her in any number of ways. Why would she do something that not only could be traced back to her, but could cost her, her new job?"

"Maybe she didn't think about that, she just wanted revenge. Maybe it was the easiest way for her to kill her. People often think that poisoning is an untraceable way to kill someone. I know from mystery shows and books that poisonings are often committed by women because it feels less personal than directly attacking a victim. Maybe Katrina thought she could get away with it. She saw an opportunity and went for it without thinking it through properly."

"But she went to all the trouble of convincing Lorraine to come here, just so she could get Margret nearby. She thought every bit of that through. Why did she get so messy with her plans at the end?" Mary smacked one hand against the other and shook her head. "That doesn't add up."

"Maybe not. But all of the evidence points to her. What might have happened between her conversation with Lorraine, until the time she put the poison in Margret's food, we may never find out. Hopefully, what we do know is enough for the police to charge her with murder." Suzie parked in front of the police station and grabbed some of the papers, then stepped out of the car. As she started to walk toward the door, she noticed that Mary lingered by the car. "Mary? What's wrong?"

"Suzie, are you sure about this?" Mary stepped up onto the sidewalk with the rest of the papers clutched in her hands. "Once we go in there and give Jason every detail, it might pretty much seal Katrina's fate. We might just give him the detail that will not only allow him to charge her, but eventually cause her to be convicted. We need to be sure, right?"

"Of course." Suzie met her eyes. "What are you thinking? Do you suspect someone else?"

"That's the problem, isn't it? There are so many suspects. Something has been bugging me since we spoke to Lorraine. If she knew that Katrina was the one who convinced her to come here, why didn't she mention that to the police after Margret was killed? She had to think that was strange, right?" Mary crossed her arms.

"Maybe she never saw Katrina at Dune House? I just assumed she hadn't seen Katrina there. She wasn't there for the dinner, remember?"

"No, she wasn't. But she has been involved in every detail of this trip," Mary said. "It seems odd."

"Are you saying that you think Lorraine could have had something to do with this?" Suzie's mind rushed back over all of the interactions she'd had with Lorraine. "I suppose it's possible. But again, she wasn't at the house during the meal, just like Freddy wasn't."

"That we know of. And the poison could have been planted at another time." Mary walked over to her. "People were coming in and out of the house most of the day. Don't you think it's possible that one of them could have slipped in and poisoned the food or drinks?"

"Sure, it's possible," Suzie agreed. "But then, how would they target Margret specifically? Look, I think we have to acknowledge that Katrina has a strong motive, she had the opportunity, and she clearly wanted Margret here for some reason."

"If you have any information that can help the investigation, you need to disclose it." Beth stepped out of the shadows near the entrance of the police station.

"Were you spying on us?" Suzie gasped.

"I was just standing there, taking a break, after being lectured by my boss, about not being too harsh to the suspects." Beth crossed her arms as she looked between them. "You obviously have information for him, and instead of giving it to him, you're standing out here discussing it." She turned toward the door. "I'll let him know that you need to speak to him."

"Okay." Suzie hurried after her and caught up to her before she got through the door. "We were going to tell him. We just want justice served, don't you?"

"Yes. That's why I wear this badge." Beth pointed at the badge on her chest. "But when I'm trying to do my job, and show him that he can rely on me, I have to deal with you interfering every step of the way. How is that fair?"

"We're just trying to help." Mary stepped up beside Suzie.

"We just want to get to the truth." Suzie glanced over at Mary, then turned her attention back to Beth. Suzie was beginning to realize she was a lot like Beth when she started out as an investigative journalist. She wanted to get to the truth and was a bit too gung ho. "Would you like to take our statement about this new information we've found? Maybe it will help you figure it all out."

"Really?" Beth eyed them both with some suspicion. "We can go inside right now, if you're really willing."

"We are." Mary started toward the door. "We have a lot to sort out."

"We can talk in here." Beth led them both into an interrogation room.

"Shouldn't Jason be here, too?" Mary glanced toward his office.

"He's off investigating a lead. Do you want to wait until he gets back?" Beth pulled out a chair to sit in.

"No, it's okay." Suzie settled into one of the chairs, then handed over the papers and launched into a description of the information they'd gathered, and how they'd found it.

"So not only did Katrina arrange for Margret to be here, but she's held a grudge against Margret for years." Beth sat back in her chair and looked up from the paper she'd been jotting notes on.

"She seems to be obsessed with her." Suzie glanced at the pile of papers. "That's pretty damning evidence."

"We're not sure why Lorraine didn't identify her in the first place. It doesn't quite add up, does it?" Mary said.

"I see what you mean." Beth stared down at the list she'd created. "As of now, I'd say we have enough to arrest Katrina."

"Even without knowing how exactly Margret was poisoned?" Suzie's eyes widened.

"I'm going to look into this more. Thank you for the information." Beth looked between them.

"Beth, I know that Katrina looks very guilty. But it's important to keep in mind that looks can be deceiving," Mary said.

"Thanks for the advice." Beth stepped out of the room. She left the door open for them to follow her out.

Before Suzie could get out the door, Jason's voice stopped her in her tracks.

"Beth! We have a problem."

CHAPTER 24

*M*ary poked her head out through the door as Suzie edged her way across the threshold.

Jason's flushed cheeks and sharp tone indicated his patience no longer existed.

"Did you threaten Katrina?"

"Threaten her?" Beth's confident voice faltered as Jason glared at her. "How? I didn't threaten to hurt her or anything."

"Did you threaten to arrest her if she didn't give you certain information?" Jason stepped closer to her. "Because the lawyer her husband hired is claiming that you threatened and harassed her to the point of tears. He claims that you told her that you had a witness claiming they saw her put the poison in the food. Is that true? Because it's news to me!"

"I, well, uh." Beth looked away from him. "She was close to cracking. I could tell. I thought if I just pushed her a little harder, she might give me the information we needed. But now, we have a lot more information that Suzie and Mary just gave me, so if you let me talk to her again, I bet I could get her to confess."

"Not a chance. I already released her." Jason sighed, then took a long, slow breath before looking back at her. "Beth, I know you're still learning, but you may have just cost us this case. You need to learn the rules and policies that have to be followed during interrogation. That's why I told you not to speak to Katrina without me present. Didn't I?"

"You did. I'm so sorry. I didn't mean to cause a problem. I just really thought she would confess." Beth hurried down the hallway away from the three of them.

"Unbelievable!" Jason walked away as someone summoned him from the other side of the police station.

"This is a mess." Suzie led Mary out of the room and out of the station. "If Katrina is the killer, she could get away with this because of Beth's mistake."

"Let's make it not a mistake, then." Mary climbed into the passenger seat, then looked over at Suzie as she sat inside the car. "Beth claimed she had a witness, so let's find her a witness. Someone at the house had to have seen something that day, whether it was Katrina or someone else that poisoned the food or drinks. There were too many people around for no one not to have seen something."

"That's true, Mary. Maybe we just haven't been asking the right questions. Let's see what we can find out. Maybe it will lead to nothing, but maybe it will turn up something." Suzie started the car as her phone beeped with a text. "Oh, it's Jason." She read over the text. "We are okay to use the kitchen."

"Great." Mary smiled. "We'd better get some essentials."

After stopping at the grocery store, Suzie drove toward Dune House.

"I know Beth has been giving you a hard time since she arrived, but I can't help but feel bad for her after the way Jason spoke to her. She looked so devastated." Mary glanced over at Suzie.

"He wasn't wrong." Suzie turned into the parking lot of Dune House. "But it isn't like him to be so angry. Clearly, this case is stressing him out.

Hopefully, once he calms down, they can work out a solution to the problem."

"You mean one that isn't firing Beth?" Mary stepped out of the car. "I thought you might be rooting for that one."

"At first, yes. But there's something about her. She has a lot of spunk, and determination. I remember feeling that way when I first started my career. All that energy and enthusiasm can lead to some pretty big mistakes. But I imagine it can also lead to a great police officer." Suzie opened the door to the house and spotted Beryl alone in the living room.

"Beryl, how are you doing?" Mary smiled as she stepped in to greet her.

"Bored, honestly. My love ran off to play with the boys, and the girls are busy knitting. Knitting, can you believe it? At a time like this?" Beryl gave a short laugh. "Really, at any time." She scrunched up her nose. "It's not my cup of tea. I don't even like tea actually. It's not my cup of coffee." She laughed.

"Coffee sounds like a great idea. Why don't I make us a pot?" Mary started toward the kitchen with some bags of groceries.

"I saw some people out on the porch." Suzie held up the bags. "I'll put these down, then let them know coffee is being brewed. It'll be a great opportunity to speak to everyone."

"I'll keep Mary company." Beryl followed after them.

Suzie placed the bags on the counter, then headed out of the kitchen and toward the sliding glass doors.

"It's a relief that they figured out how she was poisoned." Beryl looked up at Mary.

"Not exactly how." Mary scooped coffee into the coffee maker. "But they do know what was used now. We still don't know how it was delivered." She added water, then looked over at Beryl. "I think someone must have seen something, and just didn't realize it. Or maybe overheard something on the bus ride here."

"It was hard to hear anything with the racket on that bus." Beryl leaned against the counter as the coffee began to brew. "Now, that I think about it, though, Lorraine was pretty chatty with Greta. They kept it quiet and didn't seem to want anyone else to listen in."

"Interesting. You didn't catch any of what was being said?" Mary pulled several coffee mugs out of the cabinet and lined them up on the counter.

"No, they were closer to the front than I was. I

just noticed the way they were being a little secretive about it." Beryl leaned against the counter. "It's probably nothing."

"It could be something. Maybe Freddy overheard what they were discussing." Mary lined up sugar, cream, and sweeteners on the counter.

"Freddy isn't a very nice person, if you don't mind me saying. I doubt he'd tell you anything even if he heard it."

"Did he do something to upset you?" Mary filled a mug with coffee, then set it down in front of Beryl.

"He seemed friendly enough at first. He took requests for what kind of music we liked and made sure that it wasn't too loud, so that we could still chat. He pointed out some lovely scenery along the way. Honestly, I thought we'd struck up a bit of a friendship when we bonded over our experiences with birdwatching as a hobby. But clearly that was not the case." Beryl took a sip of the coffee, then smiled. "Absolutely delicious, thank you. I prefer it black, and I have tasted some terrible coffee in my time, trust me."

"You're welcome. We do our best to get good grounds." Mary tipped her head to the side as she studied Beryl. "What changed your mind about Freddy?"

"Oh, it was something so little. Most people would say it isn't even worth mentioning. But to me, it's the little things that tell me who people really are. At dinner, just before dessert, I saw Margret on the way to the restroom. She was in the hallway, and she had one of those delicious chocolate mint candies. You know the kind with the layers of chocolate and mint? They just melt in your mouth!"

"Yes." Mary tried to process the information.

"I asked her if I could have one. She told me that was her last one. She had just eaten the other two she had. She said she didn't want to eat them at the table. She didn't want to share them. She said she threw the wrappers away in the bathroom bin, so no one would know she had eaten them. She had such a sweet tooth."

"What does this have to do with Freddy?" Mary's heart raced.

"Sorry, I got sidetracked. Freddy had given them to her as she got off the bus. She said that he told her she'd been his best passenger." Beryl huffed and sucked her teeth. "Can you believe that? She harassed us the whole way."

"Wait, are you saying that only Margret had the candy?" Mary's heart raced. "That might be what poisoned her!"

"I did think about that, after the police questioned me, but I knew it wasn't the case. Margret either lied to me, or Freddy has a habit of handing out candies to women he likes, because I saw the caterer with a few of them in her hand when she brought out the cake." Beryl clucked her tongue. "He must have given some to her, too."

Mary's heart lurched. She stood up as it began to beat faster. "Do you mean Katrina? The caterer's assistant?"

"No, I mean the caterer. I think her name was Tasha. I asked her for the recipe for one of the sauces. It was so tasty." Beryl's voice trailed off as she watched Mary head for the door. "Where are you going?"

"I just need to check on something!" Mary dialed Tasha's number as she hurried toward the front door as the other guests began filtering in to get their coffee.

CHAPTER 25

Suzie stepped in through the front door just as Mary started to step out. Mary continued toward the car. "We have to go."

"What's the rush?" Suzie spun around and followed after her.

"I need to check on Tasha. She's not answering her phone. I'll fill you in on the way." Mary shoved her cell phone back into her pocket and pulled open the door to her SUV.

"Okay." Suzie rounded the car and opened the door to the passenger side. "If you're moving this fast, I know you're onto something!"

Mary started the car and backed it out of the parking space.

"Beryl mentioned that Freddy only gave candy

to Margret, and that she ate it right before she had her cake. But then she mentioned that she saw Tasha with some, too. If the candy that Margret ate was poisoned, the other candies that Tasha had might be poisoned, too." She turned onto the main street and began driving in the direction of Tasha's house.

"So you think Tasha might be in danger?"

"Yes, if Margret's candy was poisoned, then the rest might be, too. I just want to make sure that she's okay. I can't shake the idea that the candy Margret ate had to be what was poisoned. As far as we know, she was the only one who ate it, and she ate it right before the cake was brought out. It just makes sense. Doesn't it?" Mary turned into Tasha's driveway.

"You're right, it does. I hope she's okay!" Suzie hopped out of the car as Mary moved briskly up the walkway to the front door.

"Tasha!" Mary pounded on the door. "Are you in there? Hello?"

A moment later, the door opened. Tasha stood in the doorway with a puzzled look on her face.

"Mary? What is it? Are you okay?"

"That's what I'm here to ask you!" Mary felt

breathless with relief as she hugged Tasha. "I'm so glad to see that you are."

"Well, you did scare me to death! I thought you were the police knocking that hard. I thought they had finally come here to arrest me!"

"I'm sorry I scared you." Mary looked over at Suzie, then back at Tasha. "Tasha, we think we know how Margret was poisoned. Right now, it's just a hunch, but we're hoping that you can help us prove it."

"Sure, anything I can do to help, I'm glad to." Tasha peered at them. "But what can I do?"

"One of our guests said she saw you with some mint candies, on the day that Margret died. Margret was seen eating those candies shortly before she collapsed. Did you happen to eat any?"

"No, I didn't." Tasha thought for a moment, then nodded. "I do remember what you mean, though. I had picked them up because Katrina left them on the table by accident. I knew people would take pictures of Margret blowing out her candles, and I didn't want the table to be cluttered with anything. But I never ate any, I just gave them back to her."

"Did she say where she got them from?" Suzie raised an eyebrow. "Did she mention Freddy?"

"Freddy? The bus driver?" Tasha looked between them. "Why would he give her candies?"

"Someone said that he had given Margret the candy. We can only assume that's where Katrina got them. Did she mention anything about knowing Freddy, to you? Or maybe going to see him at his motel?" Suzie met her eyes. "Think about it. It's really important."

"I'm sorry, but no, she didn't mention him at all. You think the candy he gave Margret was poisoned?" Tasha pressed her hand against her chest. "Does that mean that the candy that Katrina had was poisoned, too? What if she ate them?"

"I'll see if I can reach her." Suzie pulled out her phone.

"I just saw her drive past, toward town!" Mary grabbed Suzie's arm.

"Are you sure?" Suzie tucked her phone back into her pocket.

"Yes, I know it's her. She slowed down and looked right at us. She must have been planning to come see Tasha but decided against it when she saw us here." Mary headed toward her car. "Let's go, Suzie. Maybe we can catch up with her!"

Suzie and Mary climbed into the SUV. Mary

started the engine and launched out onto the road. As she spun the wheel to straighten out the car, she groaned. "It's taking too long! She'll be too far ahead!"

"We'll catch up." Suzie patted her arm. "Just step on the gas."

Mary stepped on the gas and ignored the speed limit sign she plowed past. Suzie was surprised at how fast she was driving. Mary was usually quite reserved, Suzie was the one who often took risks.

"I don't see her!" Mary huffed.

"I think she might have gotten away from us." Suzie continued to peer out through the windshield. "I don't see her car anywhere."

"I know she was heading into town, and we would have seen her if she doubled-back. Let's just go a little farther and see if we can spot her." Mary increased the speed of the car as they neared the other side of town.

"Wait, there's her car!" Suzie pointed to the parking lot of the motel. "And there's Freddy, by the bus!"

"Do you see Katrina?" Mary turned into the parking lot. "She must be nearby."

"I don't see her anywhere. Pull up near the bus. Let's see if we can get Freddy talking about those candies." Suzie pointed to an empty spot not far from the bus.

"He hasn't been very interested in talking to us so far. How do you think he's going to react if we accuse him of giving Margret a poisoned candy? Maybe we should call Jason first." Mary parked.

"Good idea." Suzie pulled her phone out, then froze as the bus' engine roared to life. "Is he leaving?"

"Maybe Jason told the guests they could leave, since he thinks Katrina is the killer?" Mary looked over at her, then back at the bus. "He's not getting out of here without some kind of explanation for those candies." She walked up along the side of the bus and knocked on the large, glass doors.

"What is it?" Freddy popped open the doors only far enough to be heard over the engine.

"Can we speak to you for a moment, Freddy?" Mary stood at the bottom of the steps and placed her hand against the door.

"I don't have anything to say to either of you." Freddy glared at Mary. "Step back, or I'll take you with me."

"Freddy, what's going on?" Suzie stepped closer to the bus. "What are you so upset about?"

"I don't have to explain myself to you," Freddy snarled.

"We know about the candy you gave Margret, Freddy!" Mary tried to sound more confident than she felt.

Freddy's expression shifted from animosity to terror. His eyes widened and his lips parted as he gasped.

Before Suzie or Mary could say anything, he slammed the doors shut.

Mary yanked her hand back and stumbled a few steps before Suzie caught her elbow and steadied her.

"I'd say that was a guilty reaction, don't you think, Suzie?"

"Absolutely! I'm going to get Jason out here right now."

"I think it's too late for that." Mary watched through the glass doors as Freddy shifted the bus into gear.

"He's not going to go pick up the residents now. He's going to take off."

"He won't get far," Mary said.

"Mary, we can't let him get away." Suzie started to pry at the bus doors.

"No, Suzie!" Mary grabbed her arm and pulled

her back. "Don't you dare! We are not going to get on a bus with a murderer!"

The bus rumbled beside them as Freddy stepped on the gas.

"What if he manages to escape? He'll be free to hurt someone else!" Suzie glared at the bus as she called Jason.

"Help!" A shriek came from inside the bus, near the back, through one of the open windows. Katrina shoved her head through the window and shrieked again. "Help me, please!"

CHAPTER 26

"*What* is she doing on there?" Suzie glanced at Mary as she ended the call after leaving a message for Jason about Freddy and the bus. "Katrina, get off the bus!"

"He's going to kill me!" Katrina wailed as the bus' engine revved.

"No, we can't let this happen!" Mary ran toward the back of the bus.

Suzie chased after her.

"Try to get the back door open, Katrina!"

Katrina disappeared from the window just as Mary reached the back. She jerked on the handle of the emergency door.

"It's stuck! It won't open!"

"Katrina's trying from the inside." Suzie grabbed

on to the door as well.

They both pulled as hard as they could. Suddenly the door popped open.

Katrina lunged toward the opening, just as the bus lurched forward. She lost her balance and fell backward into the bus.

"Katrina!" Mary leaned in, in an attempt to grab on to her.

The bus surged forward, dragging Mary with it.

"Mary!" Suzie cried out as Mary pulled her legs up to protect them from the pavement. Suzie helped push her onto the bus. She wriggled the rest of the way with Katrina's and Suzie's help.

Suzie's heart raced. She couldn't leave Mary and Katrina alone on the bus with Freddy. She took a deep breath and launched herself onto the bus. She felt multiple hands grabbing on to her shoulders and shirt. Seconds later, she felt the vibration of the bus under her as it continued to speed up. She swung her gaze around until she found Mary.

"Are you okay?"

"I'm okay." Mary's voice trembled. "Are you?"

"Shh!" Katrina whimpered as she crouched down behind the last seat. "If he hears us, we'll all be dead!"

"I know you're back there!" Freddy's voice

carried over the speaker system. "We're all about to go on a very wild ride!" He turned on the radio and cranked the volume all the way up. "You'd better hope the police don't come anywhere near this bus, because the moment I hear a siren, I'm going to start taking shots!" He waved a gun above his head.

"This isn't good." Mary hovered close to Katrina. "This isn't good at all!"

"I'm texting Jason to warn him to keep any police cars away." Suzie poked her head up over the seat and peered at Freddy. "Maybe he'll calm down if he doesn't think the police are looking for him."

"He isn't going to calm down." Tears flowed down Katrina's cheeks. "Not until we're all dead. I've made a terrible mistake. I'm so sorry!"

"Enjoy the tunes while you can!" Freddy's laughter punctuated the pulsating beats of the heavy metal song that pumped out of the speakers.

Mary's heart pounded with fear, right along to the beat. She squeezed her eyes shut and wondered how safe it would be if they rolled off the bus through the emergency door.

As if Freddy sensed her plan, he sped up, making the idea even more dangerous.

"It's okay, Mary, we're going to get out of this." Suzie took her hand and held it tight.

Mary looked into her eyes and gave a short nod, but as Katrina continued to weep, she felt her confidence fade. They were trapped on a bus with a madman.

Suzie let go of Mary's hand and walked closer to the front. She held up her hands despite the way the bus rocked and jerked beneath her feet, testing her balance. She wanted to appear as nonthreatening as possible. Her body swayed back and forth as each pothole threatened to send her flying into one of the padded seats.

"Freddy, please! Slow down! Just stop the bus!" Suzie pleaded as she got closer to Freddy. The road was a quiet one, but Suzie hoped that no cars or pedestrians would get hurt.

"Stop the bus, so that the police can arrest me? I'm not crazy, Suzie, nice try, though." Freddy pressed down harder on the gas pedal.

"The only way any of us is getting out of this is if we work together." Suzie did her best to remain upright. "You've made a bad choice, but it doesn't have to be your last choice."

"Work together?" Freddy took a swig of his beer. "That's not going to happen. You see, everything had gone exactly as I planned. I was just about to make my getaway, when you all decided to show up and ruin everything." He glanced past her, at Mary and Katrina who followed behind Suzie, then grinned. "Well, if I'm going down, you're all going down with me!"

"It doesn't have to be that way." Suzie leaned heavily on the seat beside her and tried to keep her voice steady. "If you killed Margret, I'm sure you had your reasons. We know that she was a criminal, she wasn't an innocent victim. The police know that, too."

"That's true, there wasn't a single innocent thing about her." Freddy took the last swig of his beer, then tossed it against the floor of the bus.

Suzie jumped at the sound of the shattering glass.

"That's why you gave her the poisoned candy?"

"Poisoned candy." Katrina gasped. "You tried to kill me, Freddy? You gave those candies to me because you knew that when Margret died, I would go to the police. Because that was never part of the plan. You couldn't risk me pointing the finger at you. You decided to kill me, too."

"No. No! I wouldn't do that. I couldn't live with killing an innocent person." Freddy glanced at Katrina. "They weren't poisoned. I just wanted to make sure that you had a candy wrapper on you when the police started investigating. I figured that if they found out what was laced with poison and they found the candy wrapper on you, they would be certain that you were the killer."

"So, you wouldn't kill me, but you would set me up for murder?" Katrina hung on to her seat.

"It's just life. I wanted my revenge, so I took it, but I certainly didn't want to go to jail for it. Someone had to take the fall."

"And now?" Suzie tried to hide the tremble in her voice as she held on to the seat. "Are we going to take the fall?"

"It's too late for that, I'm afraid. The police know too much. They won't believe that anyone else is the killer. But you just gave me a great idea. Maybe we really should take the fall, together!" Freddy's voice grew louder with a sense of excitement as the bus gathered speed.

Suzie gasped as she recognized the turn he took next. It headed down a road that led to a large ravine.

"Freddy! Stop, please! You said you wouldn't kill innocent people!" Mary shrieked.

"No, I said I couldn't live with it. So, I won't." Freddy pressed the gas pedal down to the floor. "We'll all go together!"

CHAPTER 27

"*W*e need to brace ourselves!" Suzie crouched down between two seats and pushed her feet against the base of one, while her hands rested against the back of the next.

Mary and Katrina did the same.

"It's not going to matter how much we brace ourselves, if he goes over the edge, we're done for!" Katrina wept into the back of the seat she leaned against. "Phil is going to be so upset. He begged me to stop tracking people down, to just let it go, but I couldn't!"

"It's not your fault, Katrina." Suzie reached for her hand. "Listen to me, we're going to get through this."

"How?" Katrina gasped as the bus lurched, then launched over a few bumps.

Mary peeked up through one of the windows. "He's off the road now, we're getting close to the ravine."

Suzie's heart pounded as she realized Katrina was right. There was no chance of them surviving a crash into the ravine. That meant she only had one option.

As if she'd had the exact same thought at the same moment, Mary stood up and started to make her way close to the front of the bus.

Suzie followed right behind her.

"Get down!" Freddy swung the gun toward them. "Stay away from me!"

"We can't do that, Freddy." Suzie forced calm into her voice. "You're making a terrible decision, and you must be stopped."

The bus jolted, then lurched to one side as the tires squealed.

Rapid thumping followed as the bus continued to careen to the side.

Seeing her chance, Suzie lunged toward Freddy and grabbed the hand that held the gun. She wrenched it to the side until the gun fell from his grasp.

As Mary reached for the gun, the bus jerked to the side. The gun slid under a seat. She attempted to grab it as the bus swerved from side to side, but it was out of reach.

Freddy continued to try to get control of the steering wheel, even as he shouted. "I don't care how I go, as long as I go!"

Suzie tugged on his arm hard in an attempt to get him to release the steering wheel.

"Let go!" Freddy growled and jerked his arm free, which caused the bus to swerve away from the ravine, toward a wall of trees.

"Get down, everyone!" Suzie shrieked as she saw the trees through the windshield. She dropped down and braced herself against the back of the driver's seat. "Mary, Katrina, get down!" She spotted Mary crouched farther back on the bus, with Katrina beside her.

Just as Suzie expected to feel the bus slam into the trees, it rolled to a stop instead. She forced her eyes open and looked through the windshield.

Freddy smacked his hand against the steering wheel and cursed loudly.

"Hands in the air!" a voice shouted from outside the bus.

Suzie spotted Beth with her gun aimed through the windshield straight at Freddy.

"Go ahead and shoot!" Freddy turned down the music as he glared at her. "I don't care! It doesn't matter! I already lost everything!"

"We have to try to calm him down," Mary whispered. Before Suzie could do anything, Mary walked up beside Freddy. She always wanted to be the peacemaker. "She conned you, too, didn't she, Freddy? All you have to do is tell us what she did to you. I'm sure that with a good lawyer, you'll be able to prove that you had no choice but to kill her."

"You're sure about that, are you?" Freddy shouted. Before they could react, he opened the glove compartment and pulled out another gun. "Nope, not a chance. She was a little old lady, and I'm just some greasy, good-for-nothing bus driver. Who do you think is going to win in court? And when they find out how we planned to get her here? That's going to count as premeditation. There's no way out of this."

"Drop your weapon!" Beth shouted. "Hands in the air!"

"None of this was the plan!" Katrina cried. "You know it wasn't! No one was ever supposed to get hurt! You lied to me!"

"Your plan was never going to work!" Freddy scowled. "You thought just bringing her back here would be enough to get her arrested? Are you kidding? She was a professional con artist. She had escaped prosecution hundreds of times over the years."

"You told me that in order to have her arrested for what she did to me, to my family, she would have to be in the same town where she committed the crime. That's why I went to Shady Village and convinced Lorraine that she should bring the residents here for a trip. I brought her here to have her arrested, not to have her killed!" Katrina sank down into one of the bus seats and whimpered, "None of this was supposed to happen!"

"Except, that was never your plan, was it, Freddy?" Suzie stared at him as her mind raced. Hopefully, if she kept him talking they could buy some time until backup arrived. "You knew the entire time that you wouldn't be letting Margret walk away from this."

"You're right. I did." Freddy's voice quieted, edged with an eerie calm. "She took from me, so I took from her."

"Money is never worth a life!" Mary looked through the windshield at Beth. Her gun was still trained on Freddy. She hoped Beth wouldn't do anything rash.

"Spoken like someone who has never lived without it." Freddy waved the gun in his hand toward Mary. "But that's not all she took from me. You see, my life had finally taken a turn for the good. I'd met a beautiful woman. We were planning to have a family. I was happier than I'd ever been. It wasn't me that invested our money." He looked toward the floor for a second, then back through the windshield. "It was her. She lost everything. She was afraid to tell me. So she took her own life instead." His voice cracked as he spoke his final words.

"That must have been terrible." Mary tried to sympathize with him. She hoped that maybe she could get through to him.

"Margret took more than money from me, she took everything I had to live for. I didn't even know who she was until Katrina came to see me. When Katrina came to me with all of the names she had found of all of the other people that Margret hurt, I just knew that Margret had to be stopped. She had to pay with her life. I didn't want anyone else to experience the kind of grief I did. I did what I had to do to protect people from the evil that lived inside of Margret. When Katrina came to see me, she gave me the strength to do what needed to be done."

"But how?" Mary's heart raced. "How did you plan everything?"

"I've been a bus driver with Shady Village for a few years. Greta and her friends always go away for a couple of days to celebrate Thanksgiving together shortly before Thanksgiving, when most of them go home to their families. It's been a tradition for years." Freddy gave a short laugh. "This time I knew that Margret had planned to go with. She didn't have friends of her own, and she wanted to celebrate her birthday. She always wanted to be where Greta was. I think she wanted to annoy her. She lived off of upsetting people."

"She sounds terrible." Mary softened her voice.

"She was. Katrina made the plan to bring the group to Dune House for the celebration and that way she could get close to her because she could make sure Tasha was the caterer and could notify the police where she was. She was convinced with all the evidence she now had, she could get her arrested. Lorraine was so easily led. Although, I must say Dune House is beautiful. So, it wasn't really a hard sell. It all worked perfectly." Freddy smirked. "Until now."

Beth continued to demand that he drop the weapon and hold up his hands. Freddy waved the gun around, then aimed it at Beth. Suzie's heart raced. She hoped more help was on the way.

"How come Margret didn't recognize you, Katrina?" Suzie asked.

"My hair is shorter and a different color to when she last saw me. And I've lost a lot of weight with all the stress. But I guess it was really because she didn't care. I was worried she would recognize me before I managed to get her to come here. But when I saw her at Shady Village, she didn't, so I thought I would be okay. She scammed so many people, I was nothing to her."

CHAPTER 28

"*H*ow did you know that Margret would eat the candy?" Mary stared at Freddy.

"I knew it was her favorite. I found out from her sister. They used to eat them together when they were younger. It was a favorite treat their father would bring home for them. I found a recipe. They are really simple to make. Only six ingredients, well, seven, in this case, if you add the poison." Freddy gave a short laugh. "So, I knew if I gave the homemade ones to her in that packaging, she would definitely eat them. I figured the mint would help disguise any bad taste from the poison and she would eat them. I didn't care when. I just knew she would." He shrugged. "And I was right. She did. I knew she had medical issues, but I wasn't sure if the poison would kill her. I could only hope. I knew that if it didn't work, I would just have to try something else. Something more violent. Something more foolproof."

"That doesn't explain how Tasha ended up with some of the candies," Suzie asked.

"I left them on the table. I had no idea they were poisoned. I had no idea Freddy killed Margret. I thought it was Greta who did it!" Katrina stared straight ahead as her voice faded. "When I heard the way she talked about her sister, I was sure it was her. That's why I came to Freddy that night to talk about what happened. I must have dropped that notepad from Dune House at the motel when I came to see him. Tasha had given it to me because it had some of the catering details for the dinner in it, and I'd used it to take some notes. After that, I kept my mouth shut."

"Did one of you search Greta's room?" Mary asked.

"I did." Katrina raised her hand. "I searched Greta's room for any evidence, because I thought we would both get into trouble for something we didn't do, but the whole time you were setting me up, Freddy." She sank down in the seat. "How could I be so foolish? I was conned once, out of my money. Now, I've been conned again, almost into a murder sentence. I guess I'm just not very smart."

"It has nothing to do with that." Mary glanced at Freddy as he pointed the gun at Beth. "You're a good person, Katrina, and good people are vulnerable to people who have darker motives."

"Darker motives?" Freddy chuckled. "You want to see darker motives." He waved the gun in the air and looked through the windshield.

Suzie knew they had to do something, they weren't going to calm him down. She hoped he was distracted by Beth.

"Stay low," Suzie whispered and gestured for Katrina to walk in front of her toward the back of the bus. She grabbed Mary's hand and followed after Katrina. "We need to get out of here," she whispered her words. "I don't think we're going to get out of this by talking to him. It's impossible to predict what he might do next."

"Suzie, it's Paul," Mary whispered, then pointed to the emergency door at the back of the bus.

Paul signaled to them with a quick wave of his hand.

"Let's go." Mary started toward the back of the bus.

"He'll see us," Katrina whimpered.

"It's okay, stay low. This is our only chance. He's distracted by Beth." Suzie rubbed Katrina's shoulder. "We can do this, Katrina, we're going to get away."

"Okay." Katrina looked over her shoulder one more time as Freddy continued to argue with Beth. She inched her way toward the back of the bus.

"Hey! Stop right there!" Freddy turned and waved the gun at them. "Sit down. All of you."

Suzie's heart pounded as she watched him turn the gun on them.

"Drop your weapon!" Beth shouted.

"Okay, we're sitting down, Freddy. You're in charge." Suzie sat down on the edge of a seat and used her body to block Freddy's view of the rear door. Once he turned his attention back to Beth, Suzie leaned forward and whispered in Mary's ear, "I'm going to create a distraction, you and Katrina get off the bus. Understand me?"

"Suzie, what kind of distraction?" Mary hissed. "I'm not going anywhere without you."

"You have to." Suzie looked into her eyes. "Mary, I love you, and I need your help. This is only going to work if you do as I ask. Otherwise, none of us is getting off this bus."

"What are you going to do?" Mary whispered.

"I have this." Suzie opened her hand to reveal a sliver of the beer bottle that she'd retrieved from the floor. "It'll be enough to distract him."

"Suzie—"

"Mary, there's no time to argue. Please." Suzie grabbed her hand and squeezed it. "Just trust me."

"I always have, and I always will." Mary squeezed her hand back, then held her gaze for a moment longer. "Be careful, Suzie, I can't do any of this without you."

"Don't worry, you're not going to get rid of me." Suzie lowered her voice even more. "When I start walking to the front of the bus, you and Katrina head for the back. Paul will help get you out. I'll be right behind you, I promise."

Mary nodded, though her chin trembled. Her hand shook as she pulled it away from Suzie's.

Suzie watched as Freddy grew more irate in his exchange with Beth. "You're not getting me off of this bus. Your dirty trick of blowing out my tires isn't going to stop me from doing what I intended to do."

Suzie stood up while his attention remained focused on Beth. She crept toward the front of the bus. After a quick glance over her shoulder to make sure that Mary and Katrina were on the move, she launched the sliver of glass straight toward the hand that Freddy held the gun in.

Freddy yelped as the glass sliced into his skin. He stretched out his fingers in surprise, and the gun clattered to the floor.

Stunned that she managed to actually hit him with the glass, Suzie lunged toward the gun at the same moment Freddy did. She felt his weight land on top of her as she grasped the weapon with one hand. She could feel how strong he was as he tried to wrestle the gun out of her hand, but his intoxicated state made his movements sluggish. As she struggled to hold on to the gun, she suddenly felt Freddy's weight lift off her back, followed by the sound of a familiar voice.

"Bad decision, son!" Paul slammed Freddy into the windshield and pinned him there.

Suzie grabbed on to the lever that opened the doors and pulled.

Beth surged onto the bus with her gun still drawn. She whipped out her handcuffs and cuffed Freddy, while Paul kept him pinned down. Beth hauled Freddy off the bus.

"Suzie!" Paul turned toward her, looked into her eyes, and pulled her into his arms.

As Paul's warm embrace engulfed her, Suzie felt the tremble in her body for the first time.

"It's okay, you're safe now." Paul tightened his grasp on her and kissed the side of her head.

She began to relax as she savored the sensation of his hug, and the relief that his words brought. He led her down the steps and off the bus, where Mary waited to embrace her.

CHAPTER 29

*T*he scent of tea and pumpkin spice wafted through the dining room of Dune House as Suzie leaned back in one of the chairs. She felt Paul's hand still wrapped around hers and glanced over to see Mary settled on the other side of her. Lorraine had arranged for another bus and driver, and the guests had just left. They had all been shocked at the revelation that Freddy was the murderer.

It had taken some time for the scene to be processed, to explain to Jason everything that had happened, and to get permission from the medics to return to Dune House. Now that she was home, she never wanted to leave.

"Here you go." Tasha set out a tray of plates

with slices of freshly baked pumpkin pie on them. Pilot, who lay at Suzie and Mary's feet, sat up and sniffed the air. "I know it might feel impossible to eat, but you should try, and I really want you to try it. It's a new recipe."

"You don't have to convince me." Suzie smiled as she picked up a plate, then looked over at Paul. "Are you going to tell me now?"

"Tell you how happy I am that you're okay?" Paul picked up a fork and had a bite of his pie. "How it's going to be a while until I'm willing to take my eyes off you?"

"How you found us." Suzie looked him straight in the eyes. "How you and Beth ended up at the exact right place at the exact right time."

"I can tell you." Paul frowned and leaned closer to her. "But you might not like it."

"You'd better tell her." Mary picked up a plate as well. "Neither of us will relax until we find out." She looked up at Tasha and smiled. "Thanks so much for this."

"It's the least I can do." Tasha sat down at the table with them. "I'm just so relieved that this is over, and Freddy is in custody. I hope that Katrina won't be treated too harshly for her part in all of this."

"I think with Freddy's confession, she should be cleared of all charges." Suzie closed her eyes for a moment as she recalled Freddy's ranting. "Katrina really never intended to cause Margret any harm, she just wanted justice."

"So did Freddy." Mary had a sip of her tea. "But he went about it the wrong way."

"He absolutely did." Paul had a bite of pie. "This is so good."

"It is." Suzie smiled at Tasha with appreciation.

"Thank you." Tasha's smile lit up her eyes.

"So?" Suzie turned her gaze on Paul again. "What happened?"

Paul looked between Suzie and Mary.

"Beth slipped a tracker into your purse, Suzie."

"What?" Suzie gasped. "She did what?"

"She was convinced that you were going to continue to meddle in things. She wanted to make sure that you were safe." Paul lowered his voice as he continued. "And I think she wanted to make sure that she got the collar, to be honest. After her last run-in with Jason, he took her off the investigation entirely. But she was determined to prove that she could solve the case."

"So, she tracked me?" Suzie asked incredulously.

"Yes, after you contacted Jason and told him about Freddy and the bus. She heard the information over the radio and was able to pin down where the bus was and that you were on it. She couldn't get ahold of Jason, and she didn't want to spook Freddy with a police car. I couldn't find you, and when I ran into Beth in town, I asked about you. She explained what was happening and asked me if she could use my car. I agreed, if I could go with her."

"I can't believe this." Suzie popped a bite of pie in her mouth.

"Beth brought a spike strip, hoping to stop the bus along the way. When I saw where the bus was headed, I guessed that he might be going to the ravine, and we were able to take a shortcut on one of the fire roads to get there before you. We spread out the spike strip and waited. With no police presence, he didn't have a reason to be cautious." Paul caressed her cheek as he held her gaze. "It was terrifying to see that bus headed for the ravine, knowing that you were on it. I'm just so glad that you're okay. All of you. I was going to get straight onto the bus when we got there, but I was worried he would see me and shoot one of you if I did." He glanced over at Mary. "I called Wes the moment I knew you were on the bus. He was three towns away, but he arranged air support in case we couldn't find the bus. He should be here any minute."

"I know." Mary set her cup down and gestured to her phone. "He called me from the road. I told him not to break any laws. He said he had his lights and sirens on." She smiled. "We're lucky we have the two of you, and Jason, and an entire community of people here who look out for us." She looked at Tasha. "And I can't wait to celebrate that. I think we should have a dinner here. What do you think, Suzie?"

"I think that's a wonderful idea. But only if Tasha caters it. What do you say, Tasha?" Suzie smiled as she met her eyes.

"Seriously? I'm about to close up shop. Every booking I had canceled after what happened to Margret. Even if people know that it wasn't my food that poisoned her, I doubt that I can make a comeback." Tasha cringed. "I don't think anyone would show up for your dinner, if they know that I'm the one catering it."

"You don't know until you try." Mary picked up her tea and took another sip. "This town might just surprise you, Tasha. It has certainly surprised us."

"If you're willing, I'm willing." Tasha smiled. "Might as well give it one more go."

"Great, it's a plan, then." Suzie leaned her head against Paul's shoulder. "It can be a way to thank our heroes. Without Paul and Beth, we might not be here right now."

"Oh, I don't doubt for a second that you would have figured something out, Suzie." Paul draped his arm around her shoulders. "But I will always do my very best to protect you."

"We might want to thank Beth, but I'm not so sure Jason feels the same," Mary said. "I overheard him lashing out at her when we left the ravine."

"We're about to find out." Suzie tilted her head toward the door as Jason stepped through it.

Beth followed a few seconds behind him.

Pilot ran out from under the table with his tail wagging to greet the visitors.

"Hi, buddy." Jason knelt down to rub his head. "I just wanted to check on you two." He stood up and nodded to Tasha and Paul, then looked at Suzie and Mary.

"Thanks to Beth's smart thinking, we made it out just fine." Mary smiled at Beth.

"Actually, I'm here to say goodbye." Beth looked between them. "This place isn't a good fit for me."

"Are you sure?" Suzie slid out from under Paul's arm and stood up from her chair. "I think you should give it another go, Beth."

"Suzie, that's not for you to decide." Jason crossed his arms.

"She saved four lives." Suzie stared at him. "She might have broken protocol and disobeyed orders, but she saved our lives. From what I understand, she tried to contact you but couldn't reach you. So, when she didn't get an answer, she took matters into her own hands. She had a plan, she followed through with it, and even when faced with an armed criminal, she made good decisions. She didn't just threaten him, or make the situation worse by starting a gunfight, she was patient. She kept him calm until she knew that we were safe. I'll admit, I haven't always been a fan of Beth." She glanced over at the young officer, then looked back at Jason. "But now I see she just wants to get to the truth. A lot like Mary and me. I think you should give her another chance, if she wants it, that is."

"I'd like to stay." Beth looked at Jason. "If you'd be willing to take another chance on me."

"Okay, one more chance. You really did save the day. But from now on, you're under my supervision, got it? I don't want you making a move without my approval. No matter what these two try to convince you to do." Jason pointed at Suzie, then Mary. "Understand?"

"Well, I think that's a little unfair." Suzie clucked her tongue as she smiled. "What could we ever do that would get her into trouble?"

"Oh, trust me, I'm going to be far more careful around them." Beth bent down to pat Pilot's head.

"Quite rude." Mary cleared her throat and pursed her lips.

"Not inaccurate, though." Paul flinched as Suzie playfully swatted his shoulder.

"And you, sir, there's something we need to discuss." Suzie grinned as she looked into his eyes.

"What?" Paul raised his eyebrows.

"Bad decision, son?" Suzie laughed as she flung her arms around his neck and hugged him. "Someone's been watching too many action movies."

"Guilty." Paul smiled, then kissed her.

"I think I'm going to need a full explanation about that." Jason grinned as he pulled out a chair and sat down at the table.

"I'll get more tea." Tasha disappeared into the kitchen.

Beth stood a few feet away from the table and watched.

Mary looked up at her and patted the seat next to her.

"Come and sit down, Beth. If you're going to stay, you might as well get used to being a part of this wild bunch."

"I'd be honored." Beth smiled as she settled into the chair.

"Is there room for two more?" a familiar voice called out from the entranceway of the house.

CHAPTER 30

"*B*en?" Mary launched to her feet as a gasp ripped through her. "Ben!" She shrieked with joy as she rushed toward the front door.

"Oh great, you stole all of the surprise!" A young woman stepped out from behind him.

"And Cathy!" Mary shrieked again, then threw her arms around both of her children. "I thought you said you wouldn't be able to make it!"

Pilot ran in circles around them.

"We made it work." Cathy smiled as she hugged her mother back. "We would never miss a Thanksgiving with you." She crouched down and Pilot tried to lick her cheeks. "And you." She hugged him.

"I can't believe you're here! I'm so happy!" Mary squealed.

"Me, too." Suzie took her turn hugging each of them.

"We wouldn't be here without you." Ben grinned. "Thanks for making the arrangements."

"What?" Mary spun around to face Suzie. "You did this?"

"When you said they wouldn't be able to make it this year, I knew I had to make sure that wasn't the case. But they wanted it to be a surprise." Suzie winked at Ben. "Even though I warned them that you might kill me for keeping the secret."

"I think I'll let you live this time." Mary hugged Suzie, then wiped away a few tears from her cheeks. "I know, I know, I'm being too emotional. But I'm just so happy to see you both."

"We're happy to see you, too, Mom." Cathy hugged her again.

"Oh, Beth, forgive me, I'm being rude." Mary turned toward her. "These are my children, Ben, and Cathy."

"Nice to meet you." Beth smiled at them. "Your mother is an amazing person."

"We know." Cathy laughed. "Suzie never lets us forget it."

"True." Suzie grinned.

"So, where's Wes?" Ben met his mother's eyes. "I think we need to have a talk, man to man."

"Relax, Ben." Cathy patted his shoulder. "You know that Wes is a good guy, and Mom is perfectly capable of deciding who she should have in her life."

"We'll see about that." Ben dropped down into one of the chairs at the table. "I just want to have a friendly chat. Make sure he's still treating her well."

"He'll be here any minute." Mary sat down beside him.

Cathy took the chair on the other side of her mother. "Don't worry, Mom, I won't let Ben scare Wes off."

"Oh, I'm not going anywhere." Wes grinned as he walked through the door and pulled off his hat. "But I'm sure glad to see you both!" He joined them at the table.

"Wes, do you know how to arm wrestle?" Ben rolled up his sleeve and set his elbow on the table.

Mary laughed, then pushed his arm off the side of the table. "Enough, Ben! We all know how tough you are! You don't have to prove it!"

"Aw, Mom, he's trying so hard, though." Cathy leaned past her mother to poke her brother in the shoulder.

"Settle down, you two!" Mary laughed. Even in their twenties, they still had a childlike sibling rivalry that she loved watching. "I'm so glad to have everyone I love around me, but if the two of you keep squabbling, I'm going to eat Thanksgiving dinner on the beach with Pilot."

Suzie listened to the banter that flew between everyone at the table, and felt her muscles relax. There was a moment on the bus when she thought she might lose it all. Surrounded by such wonderful people, especially her best friend, she had plenty to be grateful for.

The End

ABOUT THE AUTHOR

Cindy Bell is a USA Today and Wall Street Journal Bestselling Author. She is the author of over one hundred books in twelve series. Her cozies are set in small towns, with lovable animals, quirky characters, delicious food and a touch of romance. She loves writing twisty cozy mysteries that keep readers guessing until the end.

When she is not reading or writing, she loves baking (and eating) sweet treats or walking along the beach with Rufus, her energetic Cocker Spaniel, thinking of the next adventure her characters can embark on.

You can find out more about Cindy's books at www.cindybellbooks.com.

ALSO BY CINDY BELL

DUNE HOUSE COZY MYSTERIES

Dune House Cozy Mystery Series 10 Book Box Set (Books 1 - 10)

Dune House Cozy Mystery Series Boxed Set 1 (Books 1 - 4)

Dune House Cozy Mystery Series Boxed Set 2 (Books 5 - 8)

Dune House Cozy Mystery Series Boxed Set 3 (Books 9 - 12)

Dune House Cozy Mystery Series Boxed Set 4 (Books 13 - 16)

Seaside Secrets

Boats and Bad Guys

Treasured History

Hidden Hideaways

Dodgy Dealings

Suspects and Surprises

Ruffled Feathers

A Fishy Discovery

Danger in the Depths

Celebrities and Chaos

Pups, Pilots and Peril

Tides, Trails and Trouble

Racing and Robberies

Athletes and Alibis

Manuscripts and Deadly Motives

Pelicans, Pier and Poison

Sand, Sea and a Skeleton

Pianos and Prison

Relaxation, Reunions and Revenge

A Tangled Murder

Fame, Food and Murder

Beaches and Betrayal

Fatal Festivities

Sunsets, Smoke and Suspicion

LITTLE LEAF CREEK COZY MYSTERY

Little Leaf Creek Cozy Mystery Series Box Set Vol 1
(Books 1 - 3)

Little Leaf Creek Cozy Mystery Series Box Set Vol 2
(Books 3 - 6)

Little Leaf Creek Cozy Mystery Series Box Set Vol 3

(Books 7 -9)

Chaos in Little Leaf Creek

Peril in Little Leaf Creek

Conflict in Little Leaf Creek

Action in Little Leaf Creek

Vengeance in Little Leaf Creek

Greed in Little Leaf Creek

Surprises in Little Leaf Creek

Missing in Little Leaf Creek

Haunted in Little Leaf Creek

Trouble in Little Leaf Creek

Mayhem In Little Leaf Creek

Cracked in Little Leaf Creek

Stung in Little Leaf Creek

Scandal In Little Leaf Creek

Dead in Little Leaf Creek

Scared in Little Leaf Creek

Felled in Little Leaf Creek

MADDIE MILLS COZY MYSTERIES

Slain at the Sea

Homicide at the Harbor

Corpse at the Christmas Cookie Exchange

CHOCOLATE CENTERED COZY MYSTERIES

Chocolate Centered Cozy Mystery Series Box Set
(Books 1 - 4)

Chocolate Centered Cozy Mystery Series Box Set
(Books 5 - 8)

Chocolate Centered Cozy Mystery Series Box Set
(Books 9 - 12)

Chocolate Centered Cozy Mystery Series Box Set
(Books 13 - 16)

The Sweet Smell of Murder

A Deadly Delicious Delivery

A Bitter Sweet Murder

A Treacherous Tasty Trail

Pastry and Peril

Trouble and Treats

Fudge Films and Felonies

SAGE GARDENS COZY MYSTERIES

WAGGING TAIL COZY MYSTERIES

Murder at Corgi Country Club

A Merry Murder on Ruff Road

Murder at Poodle Place

Murder at Hound Hill

Murder at Rover Meadows

Murder at the Pet Expo

Murder on Woof Way

NUTS ABOUT NUTS COZY MYSTERIES

A Tough Case to Crack

A Seed of Doubt

Roasted Peanuts and Peril

Chestnuts, Camping and Culprits

DONUT TRUCK COZY MYSTERIES

Deadly Deals and Donuts

Fatal Festive Donuts

Bunny Donuts and a Body

Strawberry Donuts and Scandal

Frosted Donuts and Fatal Falls

BEKKI THE BEAUTICIAN COZY MYSTERIES

Hairspray and Homicide

A Dyed Blonde and a Dead Body

Mascara and Murder

Pageant and Poison

Conditioner and a Corpse

Mistletoe, Makeup and Murder

Hairpin, Hair Dryer and Homicide

Blush, a Bride and a Body

Shampoo and a Stiff

Cosmetics, a Cruise and a Killer

Lipstick, a Long Iron and Lifeless

Camping, Concealer and Criminals

Treated and Dyed

A Wrinkle-Free Murder

A MACARON PATISSERIE COZY MYSTERY

Sifting for Suspects

Recipes and Revenge

Mansions, Macarons and Murder

HEAVENLY HIGHLAND INN COZY MYSTERIES

Murdering the Roses

Dead in the Daisies

Killing the Carnations

Drowning the Daffodils

Suffocating the Sunflowers

Books, Bullets and Blooms

A Deadly Serious Gardening Contest

A Bridal Bouquet and a Body

Digging for Dirt

WENDY THE WEDDING PLANNER COZY MYSTERIES

Matrimony, Money and Murder

Chefs, Ceremonies and Crimes

Knives and Nuptials

Mice, Marriage and Murder

Made in the USA
Middletown, DE
02 November 2022

13998505R00133